The Singing Blade

by

Ash Warren

**A Penelope Middleton
Japanese Murder Mystery**

For Linda and Geoffrey

Chapter 1

The Tree Eaters

As soon as the old house had stopped shaking, his first thought had been the temple.

Even without rushing to turn on the television and to check the latest reports, it was clear that the earthquake, which had struck during the evening meal he had been sharing with his wife in the living room of their old house, was going to be one of the largest to hit the area for many years. It was apparent right away that it was going to be the largest since the big Chuetsu earthquake of 2004, which, he remembered, had happened at almost exactly the same time of day when he and his wife Etsuko had been having dinner. Back then though, they had been hosting their grandchildren and their parents as well, so it had been a lot more of a worry. This time it was just the pair of them, and for that he gave a small prayer of thanks.

Just like the last time, Nakanishi had heard the frightening sound of plates and glasses crashing to the floor in the kitchen, and the lights had swung so wildly that they had smashed into the ceiling, the broken bulbs showering them with sharp glass fragments and plunging them into darkness. In addition, books and other items were scattered all around the house, and the big cabinet with the family altar and all the precious ancestral *ihai* memorial tablets had ended up strewn all over the room. Inside might have been chaos, but when they checked outside, there was also a very large crack running up the wall of the house near the front door, and part of an old cement wall at the front had collapsed onto the road.

Worst of all was the sound. When a major earthquake struck, the earth roared like a wounded animal, a deep, bass, deafening thunder that seemed to explode from the great depths of the world beneath their feet. It was *that* which really scared you, not just the sound of things breaking.

After calling his children to make sure they were all well, he started calling some of the other villagers, all men whom he had known since childhood and who regularly participated in the temple's activities. It was too late in the day to do anything now, but they would have to get up the mountain to the temple as soon as possible the next day to check that everything was all right.

Keiji Nakanishi was a tall, wiry man in his late sixties with deep-set but kindly eyes and a wispy silver beard, and even if you had never met him before, it would not have been hard to guess his profession. He had been a Buddhist priest of the ancient Tendai sect his entire adult life and looked just like he had stepped out of an old Chinese painting. He usually wore the long black cassock of his sect, but the next morning he was more simply dressed, in the traditional dark blue pants and tunic common among working men in Japan. As he had a long way to go today, like the others gathering in the little car park at first light, he wore a stout pair of leather hiking boots to cope with the rough mountain trail they were taking to the temple he administered, which lay deep in the great cedar forests of Mount Haguro, one of the ancient holy mountains of western Japan.

As the men tramped through the forest, a small bell sounded on the end of their walking sticks to warn the local bears to make themselves scarce, and every hundred meters or so up the hill they would find another larger bell tied to a tree with a rope which they also gave a good rattle as they passed by. Bear attacks were by no means uncommon these days, and the creatures had even been spotted coming down to the village in search of food, which in the old days would have been unthinkable. It seemed that climate change was having an effect even here, and the increased temperatures had meant the hibernation patterns of the black bears had been disrupted, forcing them to seek out more food and thus approach the villages more often.

Nakanishi had been the chief priest at Choji temple for nearly thirty years, a position he had inherited from his father, and which had been held by a long line of priests in his family stretching back over the centuries for nearly four hundred years. The temple lay nestled among the trees high up on Mt. Haguro in Yamagata prefecture, one of the most revered places for the Tendai and Shingon sects of Buddhism and one of the *Dewa Sanzen* or 'three holy mountains of Dewa' in the region.

These three mountains, Mt. Haguro, Mt. Gassen, and Mt. Yudono, had been sacred places for religious retreat and pilgrimage for many hundreds of years, stretching right back to the earliest days of Buddhism in Japan in the sixth century, and had forever been places where *shugensha*, or mountain ascetics, had come to isolate themselves for practice, a type of training which often lasted for the rest of their lives. Their sole purpose was the attainment of enlightenment, and the methods employed here over the centuries to achieve this were the practice of austerities of such brutal physical harshness that it had cost many of them their lives.

In this ascetic tradition, the way of his fathers and forefathers, of *shugendo,* or 'the way of trial and testing' which was carried out in the deep mountains, no practitioner was more respected in the ancient Shingon and Tendai esoteric sects of Buddhism than those known as the *sokushinbutsu.*

The *sokushinbutsu* were the rarest of the rare in Japanese Buddhism, practitioners who remained isolated in the mountains and chose to sustain themselves solely on leaves, bark, roots, and other plants, in a practice that was thought to heighten their ascetic powers, and which became known as *mokujiki*, or 'wood eating.' After years of preparation, these practices would culminate in the worshipper being placed in a specially constructed underground cell to continue their meditations for three years and three months, where they would gradually starve themselves to death in the process of self-mummification. During that time they would also eat specific plants that stripped the body of all fat and slowly poison themselves in such a way that the flesh no longer decayed after death.

After being placed in their cell, they would ring a small bell each day at an appointed time to let those monitoring them know they were still alive. When the bell stopped ringing, and after a certain period, the cell would be sealed off and not opened again for several years, after which the body would be checked for any sign of putrefaction. If this was found, the practitioner was judged to have failed the test, and his body would be buried. If, however, the body was found not to have decayed (and some people had even been greeted with a sweet smell on opening the cell), then the body would be taken to the temple and celebrated, and the practitioner would be hailed as a true *sokushinbutsu*, or one who had attained the ultimate achievement - Buddhahood in this life, and had broken the cycle of rebirth and resided forever in nirvana.

This grisly activity had been made illegal in the Meiji period in the late nineteenth century, where it had been classified as a form of assisted suicide, a practice still illegal in Japan to this day, and thus any who participated in the rite could be charged as accomplices to murder. However, even with this proscription, the practice had quietly continued, although now exceedingly seldom and accompanied with great secrecy.

Choji was the fortunate home of one of these enlightened ones, and housed the mummified remains of a four-hundred-year-old monk called Entetsu Shonin, a man who had successfully undergone the process of transformation, one of only eighteen that still existed in the country.

The remains of the revered monk were dressed in formal priestly robes and lovingly cared for inside a heavy glass box in the main hall of the small temple, where worshippers and the simply curious came from far and wide to see him and to pray for his blessing. Entetsu Shonin had been found dead still seated in the meditation posture, his legs crossed and his body bowed forward. The body seemed to have shrunk so that it was no bigger than a child's, and his face was just visible under his yellow silk cowl, his deep brown skin stretched taut across the features of the skull, yet in a way that they somehow retained a lifelikeness that almost made one feel that he was about to speak. And indeed, there had been occasions in the past where Nakanishi and others had distinctly heard chanting coming from inside the temple, only to find it deserted when they looked inside. This story had been reported in many other temples that housed the *sokushinbutsu* and was widely believed as fact.

These beliefs were hardly surprising, as you were now in the mountains of Yamagata, and people were inherently superstitious. Most people believed the mountains were haunted by *tengu*, winged demons waiting to snatch you up and devour you, and fox spirits that impersonated beautiful women and who would lead you astray if you ventured onto their lonely trails at night, stories that most people in Nakanishi's village believed as implicitly as the baseball scores they read in their daily newspaper.

This year was an auspicious one for the temple, as in a few months they would celebrate their annual festival as they always had, but with the addition of one special ceremony that was not usually performed. This year was the Year of the Ox, which fell every twelve years in the old calendar, and so the venerated monk would be taken down from his pedestal to be dressed in fresh robes, while the old ones were cut into tiny pieces and distributed to the believers as lucky charms.

The men today had a more urgent reason for making the climb, and that was simply to see if the place was still standing.

The four men, all in their late sixties and seventies, were all worried, even if none of them would admit it. They had left their cars at the bottom of the hill at first light that morning and tackled the arduous climb, first up the slippery forest path and then up the more than three hundred stone steps to the top, where the small temple rested on a level plateau looking out serenely above the tall cedars.

As it turned out, they needn't have worried. Seeing the temple heave into sight as they crested the final stairs, they breathed a collective sigh of relief. Choji was still there and looked undamaged, at least from the outside.

They stopped and rested for a few minutes, drank some tea they had brought, and then Nakanishi went up and unlocked the heavy temple doors.

As he pushed back the old wooden shutters revealing the shadowy interior, he felt a familiar presence standing next to him and heard the deep voice of his old friend Keizo Tada.

"Hmmm… that doesn't look good. It's kind of what I expected," the older man said.

Tada stepped into the main hall, and Nakanishi lit one of the portable gas lights on the floor, the temple having no electricity, and held it up high so they could see.

Several items, mainly decorations, wooden plaques, and small statues lay scattered on the floor, and the tall metal vases that usually held the flowers people brought had fallen. However, what was most worrying, and immediately visible to the two men was a large and pronounced crack running from the tatami mat floor almost to the roof in one of the main pillars in the center of the room.

The men turned on the rest of the lamps, lit a number of devotional candles, and gradually the old temple came to life again. Much to their relief, perched quietly on his raised dais, the precious remains of the venerated monk were still safe inside their large glass box, where they seemed to have suffered no damage, perhaps another sign that this was a place of divine protection, as all of them fervently believed.

The earthquake the previous evening, which had rattled the whole of the Tsurugaoka region and been felt as far away as Tokyo, had caused the collapse of several old buildings and walls in the surrounding villages, and, coupled with the damage that had been wrought nearly two decades ago by the extremely strong Chuetsu earthquake, the men had been worried about how the old temple had fared under these new stresses, and even whether it was not just a pile of broken masonry now. The ancient building, though, was clearly built of sturdy stuff. It had weathered several even more significant earthquakes over the centuries, but nevertheless, looking at the structure this morning, it was clear that the damage to the old pillars inside was more extensive than any of them had been prepared for.

A couple of the older men, who were both former construction workers and carpenters, went over to inspect the pillars, and there was a general shaking of heads that had Nakanishi worried. He was sure of one thing though, which was if anything *was* made of wood in these parts, these men could fix it. They descended from generations of timber workers, their families dating back hundreds of years to when lumber was one of the chief industries in these mountain regions of Japan, where the land was too steep and the climate too cold to grow rice. It had been their families that had built the temple so many hundreds of years ago in the first place.

Nakanishi and Tada went out to have a look at the heavy tiled roof, where to their relief, only a few tiles seemed to have come loose. However, there was extensive damage to the old earthen retaining wall at the temple's rear, and something would have to be done about that pretty quickly before the summer rains began; otherwise the whole place could end up being swept down the mountain if there was a landslide.

Nakanishi sighed. This was going to cost them a lot of money they didn't have. Not that they ever had much in the first place.

"Well, it's not too bad," said Tada optimistically, crouching down and staring at the remains of the retaining wall. "I thought it would be much worse, to tell the truth. That was pretty big last night. My neighbor lost the roof of his storehouse, which is almost as old as this place. I would say we've been lucky this time."

Nakanishi nodded. "Yep. You are right about that. It wasn't as bad as 2004 though, at least we can be grateful for that."

Like almost every Japanese, they had been long used to earthquakes of varying destructive strengths since childhood, and as a general rule as long as the roof did not come down on your head most people would hardly pause in their conversation when one happened.

Tada stood up and dusted off his hands in a gesture that meant there was nothing much to do for the present.

"I want to check that dais. I don't think anyone's been back there for years. What do you think?" he said.

"Yes," replied Nakanishi. "It's probably a good idea to check everything. We don't want it collapsing just when we have fixed everything else. And we need to move Entetsu Shonin in June for the festival, so I guess we'd better have a look."

The two old friends went back inside, where the Tanaka brothers, big, bearded men who ran one of the local construction companies in addition to their family rice paddies, were still standing in front of the central pillar, deep in conversation with measuring tapes in their hands.

"Just going to have a look at the back of the dais," Tada informed them, and Nakanishi led the way around the back of the stage to where a small door led to a narrow area behind the stage. He slid the door open, and Tada crouched down behind him with two flashlights, one of which he offered to the priest.

The older man swung his light to the floor at the base of the dais and swore.

"*Shimmata*... look at that...." he growled.

A large wooden plank just above floor level and running almost the whole length of the rear of the dais had fallen off the framework, exposing the large gap underneath. This space under the platform where Entetsu Shonin reposed was a dark void, and one which probably no one had been into in a hundred years.

Tada lay down on his stomach and shone his light into the dark space under the old dais. He saw nothing at first, but then the priest heard the breath catch in his friend's throat.

"Huh?" he heard Tada say in a confused tone.

Nakanishi crouched down next to him and pointed his own flashlight into the dark space.

"What the hell..." he heard Tada whisper.

"What is it?" asked Nakanishi.

Tada rolled onto his back and stared up at his friend, ashen-faced.

"There's a body in there..." he hissed, his eyes wide. "Inside...."

Nakanishi helped Tada to his feet and laid down on the floor in his place.

When he saw what Tada had found, Nakanishi gasped. There, in the glare of the flashlight, and just a few feet away in the dark space, were the skeletal remains of a man, dressed in what looked like a tweed suit. What the priest would never forget though, and he told this story for the rest of his life, was the pure white of the skull, turned toward them and grinning hilariously in the beam of light.

Chapter 2

An Honorable Death

One year after the strange discovery on Mt. Haguro, Penelope Middleton, a retired professor of Japanese literature who was no stranger to conferences, received an invitation to one from someone she never expected.

The investigative journalist Sal Nakamura was one of her closest friends and had once been one of her students at her old university in the ancient city of Kamakura, where she still lived. They had recently collaborated on a series of cold cases involving the world of *shogi* or Japanese chess, and while Sal was nothing if not curious about odd things, Penelope had never figured him as someone wanting to attend a conference for professional archaeologists.

There were a lot of crossovers between her field and Japanese history of course, and she had been to dozens of conferences in the past where new discoveries in ancient Japanese literature had been discussed. She even numbered among her friends several historians and archaeologists with whom she had worked in the past, but why Sal would suddenly show an interest in such an academic field was completely beyond her. Mainly he investigated crime, such as the recent *Shogi* Ripper murder case they had collaborated on, or else things like fraud or political scandals.

He had called her at 6 a.m. one morning, knowing she rose early to tend her vegetable garden, and asked if he could pop over for morning tea, a habit of hers which he found endearingly quaint and, after thirty years of living in Japan, probably the last vestige of her British heritage that was still on display between ten and eleven every day.

As always she did not disappoint, and he was happy to share some scones she had just made and even more so the jar of clotted cream she had found by some miracle the other day in one of the local supermarkets.

"You know," said Sal, after he had inhaled three scones in a row and barely paused to speak, "I think we should import this stuff. We would make a fortune," he said, pointing at the small porcelain bowl of cream on the table.

Penelope smiled.

"You could be right. But I think I might eat the profits,"

Sal poured himself some more tea.

"Yeah… I might help you do that, too. So how is Fei?"

Penelope pointed at the house next door where her best friend, Dr. Fei Chen lived with her elderly aunt.

"Been and gone. Helped me water the plants this morning and then went to work. She said she had an autopsy to perform…. I didn't ask the details, naturally."

Sal laughed. "No, I imagine not. That's not a conversation I get into with coroners like her very often, especially before meals. Speaking of the dead, that brings me to why I dropped in on you this morning…."

"The dead? That's not a band, is it?"

"No, not the band. History. A conference at our old alma mater, Hassei. I was wondering if you might like to attend with me."

Penelope looked up at him, surprised.

"And why, pray, would *you* want to go to a history conference?"

Sal smiled. "Let's just say I have an interest in this one. I think one of your old buddies is going to make an announcement about something I've been interested in."

"Which old buddy is that?"

Sal rummaged in his bag and pulled out his tobacco and cigarette papers, which he was never without, and a small flyer he passed to her.

Penelope put on her silver half-glasses which hung from a chain on her neck.

"*The Japanese Archaeological Society: Recent Findings in Imperial History.*" She read the title out loud and gave Sal a bemused look.

He reached across to her and pointed out one of the presenters' names.

"Professor Kento Suzuki," she read, and looked up at him. "Old Kento Suzuki? I thought he had passed on to that great academic body in the sky. Nice old guy. Why are you interested in hearing from him?"

Sal licked his cigarette paper and lit up with his old Zippo lighter.

"You know him, right?"

"Kento-san? Sure. We used to have lunch together sometimes. He's interested in Heian period literature, of course... it's kind of one of his fields."

"Excellent. I knew you would know him. He's a very interesting guy. We've been... in contact recently. When I told him I knew you, he said he would love to see you again. So, I thought we could kill two birds... you know..."

Penelope put the flyer on the table and poured herself more tea.

"Sure, I could do that if you like. But why the interest in archaeology all of a sudden?"

Sal shook his head and blew a long line of blue smoke out into the garden, which was just outside the living room where they sat.

"Well. It's not all of a sudden, actually. It's been something I've been interested in for a long time."

"Japanese archaeology?"

"Well… kind of. My uncle was an archaeologist."

Penelope sat up, surprised.

"He was? I didn't know that."

Sal nodded. "Yeah. My Dad's brother, Akira Nakamura. He was a professor at Keio University. He specialized in the history of the imperial family. Until…"

"Until what?"

"Until he disappeared," Sal said in a matter-of-fact tone.

Penny leaned forward.

"He disappeared? Really? I'm sorry to hear that, Sal. Do you know what happened to him?"

Sal looked out over the garden.

"As a matter of fact…yes and no. He disappeared about twenty years ago, no one had the slightest idea what happened to him. The police investigated… for years. But no joy. It was like he just vanished into thin air. And then…"

"They found him?"

Sal nodded and stubbed out his cigarette.

"They found his body. Last year. Hidden in a temple in Yamagata, of all places…."

"Seriously? In a temple?"

"Yes. Hidden under the floor. Murdered. According to the Yamagata police."

"Wow…."

"That's what I said too, naturally enough," said Sal. "Anyway, the thing is, it's a family matter. I want to know what happened to him. All my family does… what's left of them. So I promised them, I promised my Dad, before he died, that I would find out."

"I see. And that's why you want to go to this?" she pointed at the flyer.

"Yes. That's why I want to go to this. Your old buddy Kento was one of my uncle's friends. His closest friend. They worked on several papers together. And I hear he recently found something that might be interesting. Something that my uncle was working on too… before he died. So… how about it? It's this Saturday. A one-day conference. Want to come along?" he asked, giving her his most appealing smile.

Penelope looked at him and sighed.

"Of course, if you like. You know I love a mystery. Let's go. I'll give the university a call."

Sal reached into his pocket and passed her a ticket.

"Already done. I'll meet you outside the gates. Say, 8:30?"

Penelope smiled ruefully.

"I see I am in no position to refuse," she said, waving the conference ticket at him.

"No, you aren't," Sal grinned and lit another cigarette. "Now…got any more scones?"

====================

The conference hall at Kamakura's Hassei university, where Penelope had worked for so many years, was also the university's concert hall and where they held a lot of important functions such as graduation ceremonies and the like. In addition, to help make ends meet, it was rented out to various orchestras, pop bands and other organizations as a venue. It was an old building in the middle of the campus named after one of the university's founders, with comfortable velvet seats that reminded one of an old-fashioned cinema and that could hold up to fifteen hundred people.

When they arrived and took their seats a few rows back from the stage, only about half of the lower floor was filled, whereas the upstairs balcony was completely empty. All the same, Penelope thought it was still quite a reasonable crowd for an academic conference, and she had certainly been to embarrassingly worse-attended ones. Looking around the hall, she saw there were also several visiting foreigners from universities overseas, and according to the program, a couple of the papers that were going to be read today were in English, which was a pleasant change.

Strangely enough, Japan produced more archaeologists per capita than any other nation on the planet. Every year there were nearly two thousand excavation reports lodged with the government and thousands of field workers involved in a plethora of digs both big and small all over the country. This being said, the average Japanese archaeologist, like a lot of Japanese academics, lived and studied only in Japan, had no interest in overseas work and published pretty well exclusively in Japanese, making news of even quite major discoveries almost unknown in the outside world. His (or her) work was also heavily monitored by the Ministry of Education, Sports, Science, and Culture, a multi-level bureaucratic behemoth that squatted on top of academia like an elephant on a small sofa, and was without question the primary cause of most of the problems besetting the country's relatively backward education system, which below university level focused itself almost entirely on rote learning and examinations while at the same time doing almost nothing to improve the quite famous academic slovenliness of the country's hundreds of private universities.

They settled into their seats halfway through a less than tantalizing presentation from a Kyushu academic on Jomon-era pottery, and after ten minutes Penelope began to hope rather desperately that Professor Suzuki's paper, which was the whole reason they were here today was going to be a jot more interesting. The current exposition featured a seemingly endless series of slides of pottery shards from various digs followed by a long-winded explanation as to what they signified in the Great Field of Jomon History, one of the very earliest periods of study in Japan. The sight of the pottery shards did, however, remind Penelope of the great scandal which had recently rocked the usually rather sedate world of Japanese archaeology, and one of which the current presenter was probably all too aware, when it was discovered that a very well-known Japanese archaeologist had faked hundreds of discoveries around the country by planting various pieces of ancient pottery at the digs he was supervising and then claiming to have found them there. His work had been unchallenged for decades until one day his malfeasance had all come to light and a criminal investigation had been launched.

She turned to Sal when the speaker paused to show yet another set of pottery shards.

"You still haven't told me much about why we're here today, you know..." she whispered to Sal, who was sitting with his notebook on his lap and chewing sweets 'to stay awake', as he put it.

"Well, it's a bit of a long story. But your friend Professor Suzuki is one of the big names in the field of early imperial history, which, as you probably know, is pretty controversial. But it appears that it's about to get even *more* controversial. To be honest, though, I don't actually know what he is going to say, he was very hush-hush about it. Anyway, maybe we can talk to the good professor over lunch. He's up next, it seems."

Penelope consulted the program she had been given at the door.

"Imperial Burials in the Nara Basin." she read. "Sounds fascinating..."

"That's the one. I'm told he has something very interesting to say today," said Sal, offering her his bag of mints.

Penelope sighed and took one.

"I hope so... you can buy me lunch, by the way," she said with a smile.

"Oh, don't worry. It's a deal," Sal said, patting her hand.

The subject of Professor Suzuki's presentation was, as Sal had said, the Japanese imperial line, the longest imperial line in the world, (at least since the communists had put an end to the Chinese dynasties) and which traced its beginnings back to the first Emperor Jimmu, who had proclaimed the throne in 660 B.C., a day still celebrated each year with a public holiday in Japan. Among Jimmu's other claims to fame was that he was the descendant of the Shinto sun goddess Amaterasu, which had the unfortunate effect of casting some doubt on his actual existence in the first place. That being said, during the nationalist military period of the 1930s and 40s, it was dangerous even to think that Jimmu might not have existed, let alone say it out loud. In essence today, though, all of the emperors for the first eight hundred years, from Jimmu up until the end of the third century A.D. were referred to as 'legendary emperors,' meaning that there was no evidence they had existed.

Nevertheless, despite admitting this legendary status, the Japanese imperial line still maintained it began with Jimmu, and not only this, but it also proclaimed itself to be an *unbroken* bloodline going back 2,600 years, a claim regarded by nearly all serious historians as total fiction, but which was still the official government position, even though it was a little like saying that the current British monarch was a direct blood descendent of King Arthur.

After another half an hour of ancient pottery, there was a brief intermission. Sal rushed out and reappeared shortly afterward bearing cans of hot coffee from the vending machine in the lobby, despite knowing Penelope despised it, and handed her one with an apologetic smile. A few minutes later, she was relieved to see the familiar form of her old colleague Dr. Suzuki walking slowly onto the stage from the wings and taking his seat to await the Archaeological Society's current president, a rather elderly emeritus professor from a university in Shikoku, to make the necessary introductions.

A few minutes later, the president approached the lectern and tapped on the microphone. He was a nice old gentleman with whom Penelope had attended some function or other back in the days when she was a young professor, and she remembered fondly that he had insisted on paying for her as well as inviting her to his home in Matsuyama to try the delights of the local *sanuki* noodles, which he had adamantly maintained were superior to all else in Japanese cuisine.

"Ladies and gentlemen..." he intoned in a sonorous drone. "It gives me great pleasure to introduce our next speaker today, Hassei University's own Professor Kento Suzuki, who has been active in our society for over forty years now. Professor Suzuki has had a long and distinguished career in our field, and has made great contributions to our understanding of early Japanese society in the pre-Nara period. Today he will inform us of what, I have been reliably told, is a momentous discovery in early Japanese history, related to the origin of the very earliest ruling classes in Japan. Professor?"

He turned slowly to Suzuki, and the two men bowed to each other as the latter stood and placed a leather folder of documents on the lectern.

Penelope looked at Sal, who was leaning forward in his seat, and raised her eyebrows. Very curious, she thought. She looked back at the stage, and watched her old friend, a tall, white-haired gentleman in his early seventies in a dark blue suit and tie, as he arranged his papers. Behind him the screen had come to life, with a picture of a burial mound somewhere and the title of his talk above it.

She also noticed, out of the corner of her eye, a movement toward the stage from the side of the auditorium.

It was a young man, perhaps in his early twenties, wearing a long, dark overcoat that reached almost to the floor. The first thing Penelope thought when she saw him was that, given the warm weather today that he must be quite hot wearing such a coat, but then, having spent her entire adult life surrounded by Japanese university students who were nothing if not famous for their peculiar fashion choices, gave it only a moment of passing attention.

She noticed that the man's hair was cut very short, as was common for members of the various university sporting teams and athletic clubs, and that he looked muscular and sturdily built. Also, somewhat theatrically, he sported a white bandana with a *kanji* character on it that Penelope could not quite make out. This was slightly odd in a university, but quite normal for serious students sitting entrance examinations in high school, an old-fashioned custom dating back to samurai times to emphasize their sincerity.

She watched him as he approached the front of the hall, and then to her surprise, observed him leap lithely onto the corner of the stage.

Sal had also noticed him too and gave Penelope a confused glance. What on earth did the boy think he was doing?

Professor Suzuki, who was just about to speak, also turned his head inquiringly towards the sudden movement to his side.

But it was too late.

The attack came with almost blinding speed.

Moving at a run towards the professor now, the youth ripped back his long black overcoat to reveal the hilt of a *katana,* a long Japanese sword, and in three quick strides he was on top of the bewildered academic. In less time than it took to take a breath, the horrified audience saw the sword flash out of its scabbard, and with a blood-curdling scream the youth brought it down like a lightning bolt, cutting the elderly man down where he stood. The sword then arced overhead again, and a second blow whistled down, slashing open the professor's throat as he lay defenceless on the floor, and sending a spray of arterial blood across the stage.

Penelope heard herself scream, but any noise she made was instantly drowned out by a chorus of similar screams from all around her. In the meantime, the wild-eyed young man stepped over the fallen professor, knelt on the floor, and tore open his shirt. Before anyone dared or had even a moment to move towards him, he placed his long sword elegantly on the ground before him with a practiced gesture, and then, taking out another shorter sword from underneath his coat, grasped the hilt with both hands and with another hideous scream plunged the blade into his own stomach.

The whole attack, from beginning to end, had taken less than ten seconds.

Chapter 3

The Shōtō Mansion

Yuichi Kami had been summoned to the house many times in the past, yet it still gave him a nervous feeling in the pit of his stomach. He usually took a taxi from the busy Shibuya station the short distance to the Shōtō area, an upscale residential area where there were many old mansions still nestled away, although most of them had been rebuilt since the Great Kanto Earthquake of 1923, of which few vestiges remain except the annual nationwide disaster drills which still take place on the anniversary of that fateful date.

The lands in this area originally belonged to two major feudal families, the Kishu-Tokugawa, who were related to the ruling Tokugawa family of the Edo period, and the Nabeshima, the hereditary lords of Saga in Kyushu, and it was the latter that had turned the area into a place of sprawling tea fields, where impoverished samurai could find work. They called the area Shōtō, a word made up of two Chinese characters meaning 'pine' and 'wave,' one explanation of this being that it represented the sound of the wind moving through the pines, a sound which poets thought similar to the gentle crashing of the waves on the shore, and which tea ceremony aficionados thought was akin to the sound of water boiling in the tea kettle.

The man Kami had come to call upon today was a modern-day feudal lord, an elderly politician who had actually been related to the old Nabeshima clan, still living on his ancestral lands. Although this man, a rail-thin bald-pated individual named Masakichi Bando, had never held the highest office in the land, he had been, and still was, far more powerful than many of the prime ministers who had come and gone in the past. Like many faction leaders in the ruling party, he preferred to remain in the shadows, pulling on the strings of government, something he did with such skill, not to mention longevity, that his intimates in the party had long ago begun referring to him as the *kuromaku,* or 'puppet master.'

Now retired, he lived in a beautiful house surrounded by high walls and security cameras and with an ever-present corps of highly trained ex-police officers who tended to his security, eagle-eyed men who accompanied him wherever he went and were a discreet presence all around the leafy villa he called home.

But they were not the reason Kami felt nervous as he arrived today. It was their master who was the one he feared, and with good reason.

He left the taxi at the corner and walked the last few hundred meters to the entrance to the mansion, past the tall white walls to a large wooden door under a traditional tiled roof that was common in temples and as entrances to the houses of the wealthy, and pressed the buzzer outside. He knew well that the security people were not only aware of his appointment but that they had also been watching him approach the house, and, sure enough, the door instantly opened, and he stepped inside and into the presence of a large ex-special forces guard in a dark suit, who motioned to him to raise his arms while he none-too-gently patted him down from shoulder to ankle.

The guard then stood and coldly gestured for him to follow him inside without a single word being passed between them.

Once inside the entrance to the house proper, he slid off his shoes, stepped up onto the highly polished dark wooden floor, put on a pair of slippers, and was escorted by another identically dressed guard down a long passageway to the room where they were awaiting him.

The house itself felt like a relic from another age, like you were stepping back in time a thousand years to an old Japanese palace, a house built in a square around an inner courtyard garden of rare beauty, a series of interconnected traditional rooms with their sliding doors occasionally open to reveal spotless tatami mats looking out on the garden with its ornamental rocks, its flawlessly raked white gravel, its maple, cherry trees, camelia, and other flowering plants, and a pond where shimmering golden carp circled endlessly in the cold waters.

Near the end of the endless corridors, the guard suddenly stopped and gestured to him to stop, and then the man knocked quietly on the post next to the door. He heard someone inside say a simple '*hai*,' and the guard slid open the door and stepped inside.

"Your guest, sir," the guard said with a low bow to the occupant, and Kami slid off his slippers and stepped onto the shining tatami mats inside.

The *kuromaku*, a frail-looking, bald man with a long face and deep-set eyes that rarely looked at you directly, was sitting on a low chair behind a massive, highly polished low table. Behind him was a beautiful antique folding screen depicting the progress of Princess Kazunomiya along the *Nakasendo*, the ancient mountain road between Kyoto and Edo (now Tokyo), for her marriage to the *shogun* Iemochi in 1862. The *shogun* of the time, he knew, had been a distant ancestor of the *kuromaku*, and so he was aware of why this screen was often on display, to remind those who saw it of the power of the man whose presence they were in.

"Ah, Kami-san. Come and sit down. Bring tea," he ordered the guard, who silently departed for some far-away kitchen.

Kami came forward to the cushion he had been ordered to, and then on the other side of the room saw another man whom he also knew, seated off to one side. He knelt in the formal *seiza* position and bowed to the floor to both of them while offering the usual formal words of greeting.

The other man, Katayama-san, who seemed to be some kind of lieutenant that Bando favored to have with him whenever they met, also bowed, but his boss remained without moving a muscle. In fact, Kami had never seen him properly bow to anyone in the twenty-odd years he had known him.

"It's good to see you again, Kami-san," said Katayama with the thin, almost mocking smile that Kami detested. He was a tall, angular man, with a long sharp nose and watery eyes, and his remaining hair was plastered to the top of his scalp in a faintly ridiculous comb-over favored by some older men for some reason that defied most people's understanding. As they all were, he was dressed in a dark kimono and sash, as the boss preferred with his guests, Bando being famous for his profound distaste for anything even vaguely Western, especially clothing and food.

The guard reappeared with three cups of tea on a small black tray and silently placed them on the table before bowing and making his departure.

Bando, who had chain-smoked all his life, stubbed out his latest cigarette in a huge crystal ashtray and immediately lit another one from a little silver box on the table.

"Tell Katayama-san here what you know about the situation. And I want to hear any new information you have as well," he ordered in his usual soft but commanding tone and in a manner that bespoke his decades of being obeyed without question by those around him.

Kami bowed slightly at his words and lowered his eyes. He didn't dare touch his tea, that went without question as well.

"It's become more difficult since the boy's failure to finish himself, sir. There is no denying it."

Katayama leaned forward to the little silver box on the table and helped himself to a cigarette, an action which showed his favored intimacy with the boss. Kami, nor anyone else he knew, would never have dared do such a thing in the old man's presence.

"Will he talk?" he asked.

Kami shook his head vehemently.

"That will never happen. He may have failed to kill himself, but he'll remain silent. To the grave. We can trust him."

The older man nodded.

"Just like his father," he said, and Kami nodded again.

"Yes, sir."

"The boy's father was *tatenokai*, wasn't he?" said Katayama.

"Yes, he was. Just like mine," Kami said, using the opportunity to remind Katayama that he also came from a family of loyal retainers.

The *tatenokai* or 'Shield Society' had been a group of ultra-right-wing student nationalists formed in the 1960s and later led by the late writer Yukio Mishima, a man who numbered among his many achievements being nominated for the Nobel prize in literature. The 'Mishima Incident' came to be one of the most famous events in modern Japanese history when the group, which had by then become a private paramilitary organization, invaded the headquarters of the Defense Ministry in Ichigaya in central Tokyo with the intention of persuading the soldiers there to stage a coup d'état and restore imperial rule. Once Mishima had made his announcement from the balcony over the parade ground and been roundly mocked by the soldiers for his trouble, he had then retired to the Commandant's office and committed ritual suicide, plunging a knife into his stomach before having his head lopped off by his waiting second in the traditional manner.

The group had been forced to disband after the failed coup, but many of its members had retained their loyalty to its ideas, such as Kami's own father, who had spent the rest of his life engaged with right-wing causes and had been a loyal follower of the *kuromaku* right up until drawing his final breath a few months ago.

"And is the boy expected to survive? Rather unfortunate that," said Katayama, taking a sip of tea. "Which hospital is he in?"

"The Oyama hospital in central Tokyo. Under a police guard. We checked," said Kami.

"I see. Well… I suppose we will just have to trust him. But, it's unlikely we have anything to worry about if he is anything like his father."

"Yes, sir. I agree."

"Then tell us about the other matter. Any progress?" asked Bando.

Kami continued to look at the floor and shook his head. He had been dreading this question.

"We are continuing to make inquiries, sir. There appears to be no trace of the artifact at Professor Suzuki's house. We ran a copy of his hard drives, both the one that we took at the scene and also at his home and the university… but the files were encrypted."

Katayama and Bando exchanged a puzzled glance.

"You mean you cannot access them?" asked Katayama in a pained tone, like he was talking to a wayward child.

Kami nodded.

"That's right. We showed them to some software specialists we know, and they confirmed it. There is no way we can break the encryption. It's quite sophisticated stuff, and any attempt to access it improperly would result in the whole hard drive being deleted. Which, in a way, confirms what we suspected."

Bando took a swig of his tea and stubbed out his cigarette, which he rarely ever smoked to the butt.

"Exactly. It means they were there. Just as the photograph of them showed. And that they took the artifact with them. All these years we suspected it but could never prove it.... You see, Katayama? This is what we are up against. Vermin academics and grave robbers who have no respect for anything. We might not have known anything about it had that fool's work in Niigata not come to light. Twenty years we thought he had been disposed of properly. Not the case, it seems."

Katayama said something low under his breath which Kami could not catch, but it sounded like a curse.

"It's unfortunate the idiot is dead. I would have liked to have had a word with him."

Kami felt a shudder run up his spine, as he knew all too well what happened to those the thin man 'had a word with."

Bando was lighting up yet another cigarette and staring out across his beautiful garden outside, where a small yellow bird had just alighted on the branch of an ornate *bonsai* pine.

"Yes, we gave him explicit instructions to dispose of the body... and then it turns up hidden in a temple. What was Terasaki thinking, I wonder...."

"He probably was thinking about how he could wrap things up as quickly as possible without anyone being the wiser," said Katayama ruefully. "He was always a lazy little fool, and I told the Odawara boys years ago not to use him.... but... Did we get the police report? There was nothing found on the body?"

"As far as we know, nothing. The Nakamura family took possession of it, and a funeral was held shortly afterward. That's all we know."

"What about his files? His home?" asked Katayama.

"Long gone, as far as we know. He was listed as diseased more than fifteen years ago, and the widow still lives there. We've made discreet visits a few times over the years. Nothing."

Bando frowned.

"Back to square one, it seems," he said in his usual calm tone, which Kami knew masked his displeasure.

There was silence between the three men for a short while.

"Well," said Katayama. "Looks like we need to get back to work then. Find the artifact. That's the only thing linking it to the site. Once we have that, we are in the clear. And it is not like they are going to go back in there."

"Not unless the Imperial Household Agency allows it," said Kami, who had heard rumors of a change in the established direction when it came to the imperial tombs.

Bando looked up sharply at his words, and Kami instantly regretted venturing his opinion.

"Steps have been taken…" hissed the boss. "No need to worry…."

Kami gulped.

"I'm very glad to hear that, sir," he said, but he knew he sounded lame and insincere.

Both the boss and Katayama ignored him.

"And have you looked into the family? To make sure he didn't pass something on to someone?"

Katayama was glaring at him like it was his fault that his fool of a subordinate had disobeyed them all those years ago, and it was also another question he had been dreading.

"The family... yes, sir. Well... one of the nephews, sir...."

Bando was staring at him now too, which made him even more nervous, and when he got nervous, he tended to sweat. Not good. He felt a bead running down the back of his neck.

"What about him?"

Kami looked down and knew it was best just to tell him and let the chips fall where they may. He took a deep breath and said:

"He's a journalist, sir."

Katayama and Bando again exchanged a worried glance.

"What kind of journalist? Which newspaper? We have a lot of contacts, as you know...."

"He doesn't work for any newspaper, sir. He's freelance."

"Freelance? What's his name?"

"Koichi Nakamura, sir. Goes by the name of Sal...."

He looked at Katayama, whose face was a quiet mask of fury.

"Sal Nakamura...the political journalist? The *investigative* journalist?"

Bando blew out a long stream of smoke and once again stubbed out his cigarette.

"That's a name I know..." he said calmly.

"Yes, it is..." whispered Katayama. "OK. Listen carefully, Kami. I want you to watch that man. Do you understand? Carefully. Get into his house, have a look around. Make sure he is not *investigating*, for God's sake. That's not a dog I want a fight with. Not unless we have to."

Kami bowed his head to the floor again in answer.

"Come back and see us next week, Kami. Let us know how things are proceeding, said Bando pleasantly.

"Yes, sir," said Kami, bowing again to both men.

He got to his feet and backed towards the door. He slid it open and then knelt to close it behind him in the formal manner when he heard Katayama's voice from inside.

"And Kami… don't let us down…"

"Hai!" he shouted back and closed the door.

He was still shaking when he found himself on the road outside the house, and decided to walk back to the station and maybe find somewhere to have a quiet drink to calm his nerves.

He had been dreading his interview with Bando today, and even more so with Katayama, whom he and everyone else both feared and detested in almost equal portions. If he had been pressed, it was kind of hard to figure out whom he was more scared of, the quiet *kuromaku*, with his detached manner yet ruthless reputation, or his much more overtly dangerous second-in-command, a fanatical right-wing zealot whom he knew would do anything to achieve the group's objectives and protect his boss.

He found a little bar near the station and ordered a beer, which he downed in one breath and was fumbling for his cigarettes before he remembered that everywhere was no smoking these days, a fact which he had cursed long and loud in the past. He lit up anyway, and when he saw the owner look at him and then turn away, he knew his face still had the ability to scare the daylights out of most people. He wasn't a man to be messed with, and everyone knew it.

He sat glumly, smoking and looking at his empty glass.

He remembered Terasaki, the man the Odawara brothers and he had tasked with eliminating the Nakamura academic and some of the others, and cursed him and the grave his ashes lay in. If the fool had only done what he had been asked and buried the body somewhere safe, then none of this would have had to happen. What had possessed him to hide that body in a temple of all places, even if it was in some remote place halfway up a mountain? God alone knew.

And had there been anything on that body? He hadn't gone into that with his bosses, as the truth was he didn't know, and that worried him. It would be just like that idiot Terasaki not to have checked. And if there had been something, maybe even the artifact itself, was that now in the hands of the family? Or even worse, in the hands of this Nakamura journalist?

What really scared him, though, were the encrypted files. What was in them? And did someone know the password to open them? They had come up a complete blank when they had tried to access them, but it was obviously something important. Why would an academic, let alone an archaeologist want to encrypt his files?

Back in the elegant Shōtō mansion, other people were at that moment discussing the same thing.

Chapter 4

The Photograph.

Chief Inspector Yamashita of the Kamakura police had been the first senior officer on the scene at the Hassei university theatre incident, and like everybody else had been shaken by what he had seen. While there was a precedent for this killing in Japan by right-wing lunatics, the crimes had always usually been overwhelmingly political in nature, and the victims, naturally enough, were usually lawmakers of some stripe. For one of these people to kill an archaeologist was, if nothing else, new, and the chief inspector was very curious as to the motive for such a bizarre act. The problem was that the perpetrator, a young student named Hisafumi Odawara, had not uttered a single word despite being conscious now in the hospital for several days.

Apart from the surprise of the incident himself, he had been even more amazed to find among the audience members that had been detained to make a statement, two of his oldest friends, and he had made sure they had been processed as soon as possible and sent on their way.

A week later, though, he was invited to dinner at Penelope's house, where Sal and Fei joined them. He and Fei also usually met once a month to play *shogi*, the game of Japanese chess, so they were also very old friends and had worked together for many years.

Penelope had made her beef stroganoff again, which she knew was one of Yamashita's favorite dishes, and Sal had supplied a nice bottle of Californian cabernet to go with it.

After the meal, Yamashita got down to business though. Naturally, everyone had a lot of questions for him about the case, but Yamashita had his own as well.

"So, Sal. First things first. Tell me, why were you and Penny-*sensei* at that conference? You don't look like a man with much of a thing for digging up old bits of pottery and the like." he said with a smile.

Sal nodded. "Yeah, normally you'd be right about that, but in this case, it was just the opposite. As I've already explained to Penny-*sensei*, Professor Suzuki was an old friend of my uncle, who as you know, was also murdered. You remember I told you about that a while back?"

Yamashita nodded. "Yes, of course, I remember. That was in Yamagata? My condolences, by the way. That was quite a shocking discovery."

Sal gave him a little bow of thanks. "Anyway, I suppose the question you've got is why on earth a right-wing nutter like the Odawara kid wants to kill a professor of archaeology? Well, I had the same question about my uncle, who was also a professor of archaeology. Why would anyone want to kill him? And of course, what's running through my head…is there any connection to the death of Professor Suzuki, like twenty years later? I mean, how many archaeologists do you know who meet grisly ends like that?"

"Good question. As you know, I'm a cop. So, I don't believe in coincidence," asked Yamashita. "Are you going to venture a guess?"

Sal rolled himself a cigarette and lit it.

"Right-wing loonies kill for political reasons, right?" he said looking up at the ceiling and meditatively watching the smoke from his cigarette curl into patterns.

Yamashita nodded. "That's the usual MO."

"So, you tell me, chief inspector. History. Politics. Is there any historical or political controversy that stirs up the hornets in this nest?" asked Sal.

Fei looked up at him with interest.

"Of course, there is. These guys are obsessed with the past. With the war, for example. All that sort of thing. They are all reactionaries at heart. They believe in the good old days when the emperor was divine, and all was right with the world. It's still something they believe, and that's still a problem for this country's neighbors. You know, the ones they invaded. And half the government still troops off to pray at Yasukuni shrine every five minutes and thinks there's nothing wrong with it."

Fei was referring to the controversial shrine in central Tokyo where many people still went to pay homage to the millions who had died in the war and those who had served the state since the 1860s. Unfortunately, much later, the shrine had also seen fit to enshrine the spirits of many Class A war criminals from the Second World War, so now any visit to the place was seen as highly insensitive to Japan's neighbors, like China and Korea, which had fought Japanese colonialism both before and during the war. At the same time, however, it had also made the shrine a focal point for right-wing activists and politicians from the ruling party, who, while they were ostensibly visiting the shrine to 'pray for peace,' ran the risk of having their action seen by other countries as the equivalent of visiting Hitler's grave to lay flowers.

Sal blew a long stream of smoke out the door into the darkened vegetable garden, where two of Penelope's cats watched it pass over their heads.

"Exactly," he said, looking at Fei. "Before Suzuki's unfortunate death, we had no idea that there was an area of archaeology that might be a catalyst for the right-wing to take some kind of action. It's very interesting. And what I think is very simple: I think both the killings are related to it. Both my uncle and Suzuki."

"What area of archaeology are you talking about? I mean, it's nothing to do with the war. I still don't follow you," said Penelope.

Sal nodded. "You're right. It's nothing to do with the war. But it is to do with the imperial system. The reason we fought the war, you remember. It was sold to the Japanese public as the emperor stretching out his protective hand to the nations of south-east Asia, to guard them against the evil western powers who wanted to come and snatch their countries. The emperor is at the center of what these fanatics believe is important. The symbol of all that is good in this country. And both my uncle and Suzuki were specialists in the history of the imperial line."

"But that's *ancient* history. Why would a right-wing nutcase today want to kill someone over pottery?" asked Penelope, returning from the kitchen with dessert.

"Another good question. My uncle and Professor Suzuki were old friends, you know. They worked on several projects together. There were a number of joint papers published by them back in the day. I think… that they were involved in something together, and probably my uncle was the more dangerous of the two back then. Or maybe they just were not aware of Suzuki's involvement up until recently. But whatever it was, I think the same people killed both of them for the same reason."

"OK. I'll play," said the chief inspector. "There might be some similarities, as you say. But I still don't get the connection between archaeology and these people. What's the hook?" asked Yamashita.

Sal smiled grimly.

"Tombs."

The was silence in the room for a few seconds.

"Tombs?" repeated Fei with a surprised look.

Sal nodded.

Penelope served them all a plate of tiramisu. "I think I see where you are going with this. The imperial tombs, you mean?" she asked.

Yamashita's fork stopped midway to his mouth. "You mean the imperial tombs… like that big one in Nara?"

Yamashita was referring to the *kofun* or burial mounds in Japan, the enormous 'keystone' mounds in the ancient capital.

"I thought they were closed to archaeologists," Fei said.

Sal stubbed out his cigarette and took a mouthful of tiramisu.

"This is delicious as usual, Penny-*sensei*. Yes, they are. The Imperial Household Agency has never permitted any official investigation of an imperial tomb. They say it's sacrilegious. And the right-wing who run the government agrees with them."

"So…." said Yamashita. "What's the issue with the right-wing then? Was Suzuki asking permission to dig up a Japanese emperor?"

"I think he was. And that's motive enough for these wackos. But I think there is more to it."

"What? Something your uncle was involved in?" asked Yamashita.

"Yes. Exactly. I mean, think about it for a minute. These tombs, the imperial tombs, which are all over Japan. These things are like the bloody pyramids. Perhaps full of priceless artifacts. The Japanese emperors could have been very like the Chinese emperors in that way. They were buried with considerable treasure. At least, that's the idea the historians have. But as no one has ever been allowed in to dig them up and do a proper investigation, no one really knows. Just imagine that you live in Egypt for a moment, and the government has never allowed anyone to enter a pyramid. Or excavate a place like Pompei. It's completely bizarre, that's what it is. The government doesn't seem to want you to know your own history."

Penelope nodded. "You're right, it does sound very strange. But the Imperial Household Agency would have turned down any request like that. They are in sole charge of the tombs. They always have in the past, anyway."

Sal smiled his usual slightly goofy smile, and cleaned his thick glasses with a handkerchief.

"Yep, in the past, they have. But I think 'the times they are a changin'' as Dylan said. And there is a rumor going around that they may have authorized a limited excavation of some of them. So the chatter goes anyway. And Suzuki and his team would have been first in line for that..."

"Why them?" asked Yamashita.

"Because Suzuki and my uncle were leading experts in that field, and they have been petitioning the IHA for years. The imperial history and the lineage of the emperors, that was their main area of study. But to tell you the truth, I think they were up to something long ago, way before the IHA even thought about giving anyone the green light to go in."

"Seriously?" said Fei. And what might that have been?"

Sal reached into his bag, drew out a large yellow manilla folder, and laid out a set of faded black and white photographs on the table which the others gathered around to see.

"This is secret, OK? I don't want anyone outside of this room to know I have these."

"What are they?" asked Yamashita.

"Well...." said Sal. "Whoever murdered my uncle must have been in a hurry, and they didn't bother to check his coat pockets. After the autopsy, which showed he died of strangulation by the way, the family was given his possessions, which were just his clothes and whatever he had, which included a packet of photographs, you know, like the kind you used to pick up at the camera shop after you had them developed. This was found in his jacket pocket. Anyway, it was pretty damaged with mold and damp and the like, but I was able to get these four photos out of it, and I had them blown up."

Penelope held up one of the photographs, which showed a group of six men all dressed in casual clothes standing on what looked like a small rise in a forest.

"Do you know who they are?" asked Penelope.

Sal nodded. "Yes. It's taken of going back and forth too. The film is about twenty years old, so it's hard to recognize these guys now. But these two, that's my uncle and Professor Suzuki."

"They certainly look much younger than…." said Yamashita.

"So do we all," said Fei, glumly.

"What about the others?" asked Penelope.

"That's where it gets interesting. The other five guys, and presumably the guy taking the picture, are all archaeologists, research students, mainly from Hassei, Kyoto and Osaka universities. They were all specialists in Nara and pre-Nara period Japanese history, so…. the sixth century and before."

"The beginning of the early imperial line then," said Yamashita.

"Yes," said Sal. "But there is one more thing."

"What's that?"

Sal paused and looked around the table.

"They're all dead… or missing."

=====================

There was silence around the table for a moment while the little group of friends took in Sal's words.

"All of them?" asked Yamashita.

"All of them. Including, but not confirmed, the guy with the camera. We dunno who that was. Anyway, these three," said Sal, pointing to some grainy figures in the photograph, "met untimely deaths. This guy was run off the road on his bicycle, cycling home from work at night, a hit and run. This one 'fell' from the balcony of his apartment the day after he got married, so a rather unlikely suicide. This one, a competitive swimmer who was apparently in the running to go to the Olympics when he was a student, 'drowned' while out fishing. And these other two disappeared mysteriously, all within a few months of this photo being taken. Including my uncle. And Professor Suzuki, had the most dramatic end of all of them…."

Yamashita looked at Sal.

"Well, point number one Sal, you can't keep this to yourself. There needs to be a police investigation. It appears no one has put this together before. But you're talking about mass murder here. And there are probably multiple missing person investigations that we don't know about, which ties them together."

Sal shook his head.

"Look, I knew you would say that, and it's fair enough. But I am asking that you keep it under the radar for the time being. There are a few things I want to follow up on quietly before we go and let whoever has been doing this in on the fact that they are being identified. Do you think you can manage that?"

Yamashita looked up at the ceiling and gave a grim smile.

"Yeah... perhaps. But you know the police, the place leaks like a sieve."

Sal laughed. "Yes, believe me, I'm a journalist. I know that...."

"But anyway, I will do my best. For the moment, only I know about this, so I see no reason that has to change. As long as you keep me abreast of what you are doing. Is that a deal?"

Sal put out his hand and they shook.

"Deal," he said.

"OK then. Now it's my turn to tell you something, since we are all sharing here," said Yamashita.

"Oh... good. What?" asked Fei, who had retired to one of the wicker chairs next to the little wooden verandah that looked out over the vegetable garden to smoke her antique Japanese pipe.

"As you know, we are investigating Professor Suzuki's killer, who is one Odawara Hisafumi. He's very interesting, even though he has refused to talk to us. But we've managed to find out quite a bit about him, and even more interestingly, his family. This ties very closely with what Sal was talking about earlier, that there might be a connection to the ultra-right."

"Go on, this is something I have been suspecting too," said Sal, leaning forward with this chin in his hand.

Yamashita smiled.

"Young Hisafumi, it appears, has had a fascination with sharp things since his earliest days. His papa, for one, is an *iaido* master. That's for a start," he said.

"*Iaido*?" asked Fei. "That's a new one on me."

Yamashita smiled sympathetically. "Yeah, it's not that well known. But it's probably one of the strictest martial arts in Japan, yet nowhere near as famous as many of the others, like *kendo*, which most sword aficionados practice. There's a lot of overlap, though, and many of the *iaido* guys also practice *kendo* at a high level."

"It's a favorite with certain elements of the martial arts community, especially the very conservative ones," said Sal. "It's generally known as 'the art of drawing the sword,' but a better translation would be 'a way of presence and action.' It's a practice that is supposed to develop the perfect warrior, one who's always ready to act and always in perfect moral harmony, a combination of someone who is an intellectual aesthete and also a man of action. So, it leans into the idealized cult of the samurai warrior, you know, *bushido* and all that, which was popular in the late 1890s and later into the military period. The difference with *kendo,* though, is that these guys use real swords, not bamboo *shinai.*"

"Isn't that dangerous?" asked Fei.

Yamashita shook his head. "Yes and no. Mostly it is performed as *kata,* a solo exercise in the *dojo* against an imagined opponent, so I imagine that saves a lot of injuries…."

"Well, that's good to hear," said Penelope optimistically. "So how does this relate to our suspect, young Hisafumi? Is his family involved? The father?"

Yamashita took a sip of his white wine.

"He may well be. The father, who runs his own *iaido* and *kendo* school in Tokyo, was a member of the *tatenokai* back in the early 70s when he was a student at Waseda university."

Penelope gave a sharp gasp of exclamation, and Fei looked at her, puzzled.

"So, are you going to tell us, Penny?" asked Fei.

Sal smiled. "I knew if anyone knew that name, it would be a literature professor."

"It's not a word I've heard for a very long time. It means Shield Society. I don't know much about the group, just that Yukio Mishima took it over, that it was a right-wing student group and that most of the members came from Waseda. That's all I know. Was the father part of the group that took over the Self-Defense ministry campus with Mishima?" Penelope asked.

"No. He wasn't there that day, which probably kept him out of jail. But he was a very involved member of the organization. Apparently, he made up for his absence that day with a long criminal record and a couple of short stints inside for assault. Why we allow a nutter like him anywhere near swords is a bit of a failure on our part, I think."

"I agree," said Sal. "But I think you can safely assume he and his buddies made sure young Hisafumi was thoroughly radicalized as a boy, and more to the point, it directly connects these guys with whatever Professor Suzuki and his buddies were up to."

Penelope topped up their wine glasses.

"So, what *were* Suzuki and your uncle up to? And where was this picture taken?" asked Penelope.

Sal sighed. "That's the million-dollar question. We know Suzuki and his friends had been petitioning the Imperial Household Agency to let them open up the tombs. Or at least one of them. We also know he was going to make some big announcement that day."

"So, what was it? You have his lecture notes, don't you?"

Yamashita shook his head.

"Actually, no. We don't. He had them on a flash drive. And it was taken by someone on that stage."

"You're kidding," said Fei.

"I'm not," sighed Yamashita. "Everything was on that drive, and his computer was also taken. He was a very cautious man, for some reason. We went to his home and searched for it, and we found another computer, but the hard drive had been wiped. It looks like someone had beaten us to the punch yet again."

"Wow…." said Penelope. "I wonder what he was going to say."

Sal stubbed out his cigarette and leaned forward. He tapped his finger on the photograph of the men standing on the little rise in the forest.

"I'm going to hazard a guess. I think he found something. In fact, I think *they* found something. I think this picture was taken at one of the imperial tombs, and I think these guys had been *inside it*."

"Inside an imperial tomb? But surely that's…."

"Highly illegal," said Sal. "And highly offensive… to certain people."

Yamashita gave a low whistle.

"Why would a group of highly respected archaeologists and academics do such a thing though, Sal?" asked Penelope.

Sal shrugged.

"Simple. They couldn't resist."

Chapter 5

The Stone House

The next morning Penny was having breakfast, while at the same trying to dissuade the inappropriate interest two of her cats were showing in the jam on her toast, when the phone rang.

"God, who's that this early?" said Fei, looking up from her morning newspaper.

Most mornings just after dawn Fei would come in from the next-door house where she lived with her elderly aunt, and the two women, who were both emphatically early risers, spent an hour working in the vegetable garden, particularly in the summer when it was only cool in the mornings and when there was a riot of summer vegetables that needed tying, pruning, harvesting or some other task.

"Hello, Sal," said Penelope as soon as she lifted the receiver.

"How did you know it was me?" asked Sal after a pause.

"Because you are the only person I know up at this hour who has my number. And I got the impression last evening that you wanted my help with something."

"Hmmm…Very impressive powers of deduction, Sherlock."

"I know. Imagine what I could do if you gave me time to have coffee."

Sal laughed. "OK, I'll try to remember that. Anyway, sorry about the early call, but yes, I was wondering if I could borrow your eagle eye for a few hours."

"Oh? Is this another bird-watching trip in Nagano? Fei and I aren't going there again until you install a proper bath, you know."

A few years ago, Sal had bought a ramshackle old house in the mountains of Nagano, which he used whenever he could, and had often invited Penelope and Fei there, where they had seen a number of very interesting birds (ornithology being a recent interest of Penelope's) during their walks, and also nearly laughed themselves to death watching Sal's attempts to light a fire to heat the water for the ancient bathtub that still existed there.

"Unfortunately, there's no time for birds today. I want you to come with me to my aunt's place."

"Your aunt?"

"Yes, my Aunt Yoko, my late uncle's widow. I want to look at my uncle's papers and see if there is anything that might be useful. I thought it might be good to have an objective opinion. What do you think?"

Penelope paused.

"Are you sure your aunt doesn't mind a perfect stranger looking through her late husband's possessions?"

"I think it'll be OK. The police have already been through the place. And they didn't find a thing, but that's not unusual for the police. And don't tell Yamashita I said that either....."

"OK, I won't. What time do you want to go? I gather this is today?"

Sal picked her up in his incredibly filthy old Toyota Landcruiser a few hours later and they arrived at his aunt's old home in the beach suburb of Yuigahama not long afterwards, Kamakura being a small town and relatively easy to get around if you knew your way and avoided the center of town. The city, which was a warren of tiny streets after many centuries of totally unplanned development, had once been the capital city of the first *shogun* in the late twelfth century and had rejoiced in being known as the administrative center of the country for around two hundred years before the center of power once again shifted back to Kyoto. All that remained today of its former glory were the many Zen temples and shrines favored by the *shoguns*, but which had the advantage of making the city one of the most picturesque and interesting places in the country, and giving it the nickname of 'little Kyoto.'

One of the main reasons the ancient military leaders had chosen this area to develop their city was because it was by the sea, which meant it was easy to bring in food, arms, and other important articles, and it was still favored as a seaside place by the many tourists who flocked to its beaches, especially in the summer.

Sal's Aunt Yoko lived very close to Yuigahama, one of the largest and most popular of the city's beaches and not far from the famous Hase and Kotoku-in temples, which were two of the most important tourist attractions.

The now elderly lady lived in an old wooden house at the end of a tiny alley off the main road that led up to Hase temple in an old house, not at all unlike the one that Penelope owned on the other side of town. She was a sprightly, white-haired woman who still wore her hair long and most days had a long ponytail trailing down her slender back.

She greeted her nephew warmly, and Penelope could tell they had a close bond and knew that Sal had kept in fairly constant contact with her over the years.

She immediately ran off to the kitchen to make some tea, and Penelope and Sal lit a candle and prayed at the family altar, which had a large picture of her husband adorned with a black cloth.

"It must have been an awful shock to her when they found the body after all these years," Penelope whispered, and Sal nodded.

"Yes, but I think the whole family felt more relief than anything else. We knew he was dead, of course, he was not the type of man who would ever just disappear, but the not knowing what happened to him was the worst. At least that's over for her now."

Aunt Yoko bustled into the room with tea and sweet bean-paste cakes, and made them sit at the low *kotatsu* table in the living room.

"It's always nice to see Sal," she said with a smile. "He's been looking after me since he was a boy. Ever since Akira left us," she said, glancing at the altar.

"You are lucky to have had such a supportive family," said Penelope. "I can't imagine what it must have been like,"

The older woman nodded.

"Well, it is what it is. At least he can be at peace now. And his family, too," she said firmly.

They sipped the strong green Shizuoka tea she had served and talked about family things (how cute Sal had been as a small child), living so close to Hase (unbearable with all the tourists), and other matters until Sal finally broached the reason for their visit.

"His office? You want to look in there?"

"If that's all right with you. I'd like to see if there is anything the police missed."

She nodded and, after they had finished their tea, led the way down a small passageway to the rear of the house.

"Well, they weren't in here very long, you know. They just had a quick look around. Of course, I kept it the same. The same way he left it that day. I just closed the door and never came in here…" she shuddered slightly.

"I'm sorry," said Penelope. "This is very intrusive, I know. Sal seems to think your husband may have been working on something important. Maybe that's why…."

"Yes… I know. I thought so too. Especially after the break-in. I mean, that kind of thing seems to happen all the time now, but back then, well…I did wonder…."

"The break-in? What do you mean? When did that happen?" said Sal, looking up quickly from the pile of papers he was going through on the desk.

"Oh, well. It was just after he went missing. They didn't take anything, but I know they were in here. Things had been moved around. Things your uncle wouldn't have touched. I can't imagine what they were looking for, if they were looking for anything at all, that is," she said.

It was an old-fashioned tatami mat room with a low table and chair where the professor had worked. Pens and books covered the desk, and there was a huge crystal ashtray that was still full of cigarette butts and which she had not had the heart to clean.

"Did you report it to the police?"

"The police? Oh yes. At the time, they came and looked around, but like I said, nothing seemed to be missing. Maybe something disturbed them. They didn't even take any of my jewelry, and that was just sitting on the table in the bedroom....."

Sal and Penelope exchanged glances.

"That does seem rather odd," said Sal. "Has there been any other break-in? Anything else you noticed?"

"No, nothing at all. Anyway, you help yourself and have a good look around. Stay as long as you like, and I'll go and make some more tea."

She left them alone, and Sal and Penelope began looking through the myriad of papers and the overflowing filing cabinets.

After about twenty minutes, Penelope had a sneezing fit because of all the dust and stepped into the doorway to breathe when Aunt Yoko appeared with two cups of tea on a small tray.

"I thought you might prefer some cold tea. It's pretty warm today, I can't believe it's almost autumn…" she said, and put the tray down on the table.

"Yes, even for October…." said Penelope. And this room… it has no windows, does it? And no air conditioning. It must get really hot in summer."

"Oh, yes. That's right. Akira always said he hated working in this room in the summer."

Penelope picked up another folder, and then she stopped and shot Sal a look, but he was busy going through the bookshelves.

"So, Yoko-san. Where did Akira like to work in the summer?"

Aunt Yoko smiled. "Oh, in summer, he always worked in the *kura*. It's much cooler. He set up a little office out there. That's where he spent most of his time when it was hot...."

Sal's hands froze on the book he was holding, and he turned quickly around.

"You have a *kura*?"

"Of course. What are you talking about..." she laughed. "Don't you remember? You used to play hide and seek in there with your sister when you were little. Akira turned it into his office in the summers...."

Sal looked at Penelope, who was smiling.

"Can we see it?"

"Of course. It hasn't been opened in twenty years, though. It must be even dustier than this place...." she said, waving her hands at the less-than-imaginary dust motes.

She led them to the back door of the house and out into her rather unkempt old garden, which she clearly only used as a place to hang out her washing, and sure enough, in the corner of the property was one of the large, white stone-walled storerooms with a heavy grey tiled roof, a place which in the old days had been used to store foodstuffs and the family valuables, its meter-thick walls and heavy metal doors making it impenetrable to any but the most determined of thieves.

"Wow," said Sal. "I'd completely forgotten about this place. And Uncle Akira used to work in here?"

"Oh yes, every summer. He was working here before he died, that was in summer too, I remember…."

Sal approached the heavy iron door that was red with a century or more of rust.

"Is it locked?"

"No, we lost the key years ago. But the door might be a bit hard to move. You can try if you like, but don't hurt yourself…."

Sal grasped the heavy ring on the front of the door, and after a couple of determined yanks, it moved slowly to a half-open position that allowed them to slide inside.

"That door was always a problem. I'll have to get it fixed…" said Aunt Yoko. "Anyway, just feel around. There's a light inside; the switch is just next to the door."

Sal and Penelope stepped inside, and a second later the little storeroom was lit by a single bulb that swayed on the end of its cord from the center of the ceiling.

As Aunt Yoko had said, it was set up like an office. There was a large Western-style desk and chair, an old typewriter in the center of the table, and several bookcases and filing cabinets, very similar to his other office in the house.

"No one's been in here since he died. Even the police didn't bother checking it. Do you think it may have what you are looking for?" she asked. Sal thought she sounded a little excited, but looking around, he sighed.

"Well, you never know. We'll have a poke around if you don't mind."

Aunt Yoko nodded. "Well, of course, dears. Please take your time."

She left them to go and see about lunch, and Sal and Penny began to search through the folders and other papers that lay everywhere.

"She's right about one thing, it's much cooler in here," said Penelope.

"Yeah, you're right. It must be about ten degrees cooler than inside. No wonder he liked being out here. Still… I wonder if it was not Mosquito Central," said Sal, pointing at several burned-out mosquito coils lying around the floor.

Sal went straight for the filing cabinets, some of which he had to force open with an old metal bar, as they had been almost rusted shut after all the years of being unopened, while Penny started looking through the folders on the desk.

After about fifteen minutes of rifling through folders of papers and ancient students' essays, a small blue object in the wastepaper basket caught her eye. She reached down and recognized it at once. Carbon paper. A thing that straight away drew her back to her childhood and afternoons hanging around her father's office with Miss Jenkins, his secretary, who always took her out for ice cream sundaes at the department store around the corner.

She took it out and carefully unfolded the fragile old navy-blue paper to reveal what looked like a part of a letter.

"What do you think about this?" she asked Sal, who stopped what he was doing and came and stared at the paper over her shoulder.

"Wow. Carbon paper. I remember that from when I was a kid, but I've never seen anyone use it. From the typewriter, right? My dad used to have that back in the day."

"I used to use it when I was a student, which tells you how old I am. If I'm not mistaken, this is a part of a letter to someone named Sakaki. He appears to have been a colleague."

Sal paused and thought.

"One of the men in that photo was a Tomohiro... Tomohiro Sakaki. I think he was a research student at Keio, my uncle's old university. He was one of the guys who disappeared around the same time... Yeah. The swimmer..."

Penny raised her eyebrows. "That's odd. Listen to this:

The artifact's provenance may be impossible to determine accurately, and the age. However, it shows no similarity to anything that has been found in similar excavations in Japan from this period or....

"Or what?" asked Sal.

Penelope shook her head. "I have no idea. That's where it breaks off. It looks like it was a page of a letter which he decided to change and maybe start again.

Sal reread the fragment of the letter. "I wonder if he was about to say 'place'... 'period' or 'place.' That would make sense...."

Penelope nodded. "It would. It would make perfect sense."

Sal slapped his thigh. "This is what I thought all along. They found something.... They found something, and they didn't really understand what it was. But they knew it was important."

"Important in what way, though?"

"Well, important enough to make someone want to get rid of you. And any of your friends that had seen it."

Penelope looked at Sal sympathetically. He was obviously desperate to find some key to his uncle's death, and his journalist's mind was clearly reaching at any straw that floated past.

"Sal, that's true, but look. He was an archaeologist. This letter could be referring to anything."

Sal looked at the floor, downcast.

"I guess that's true. It's just that it was written to Sakaki, the same guy that was with him in the photo, his student who also went missing. That's a bit of a coincidence, wouldn't you say?"

Penelope shrugged. "Perhaps. Let's keep this piece of old carbon paper anyway. It brings back memories for me too…It might be something… it might not."

"OK, anyway, let's keep looking. Maybe there is something else in here…" Sal said as he started breaking open another of the old filing cabinets.

Penelope went through the rest of the papers and folders piled on the desk and then started on the drawers that ran down the side. The top one was filled with old bottles of ink, bits and pieces of stationery and carbon paper, like the one she had found before. The second had a pile of old papers from various European scientific journals, some of which the professor seemed to have contributed to.

The third draw was locked.

She shook the handle hard, but it wouldn't move.

"I wonder what you have in here…" she muttered to herself.

She looked around and found an old paper knife on the desk, and after about a minute of wrestling with the lock, she felt it move in an anti-clockwise direction and the drawer opened.

Inside was nothing but an old pink manilla folder, which she opened.

It was empty.

"Damn. I wonder what was so important you locked this up for."

She looked over at Sal, who was sitting cross-legged on an old dusty rug looking through a pile of hanging folders from one of the cabinets. She pulled the paper knife she had used to force the lock from where it was protruding, and it dropped on the old stone floor and bounced under the chair.

Penelope pulled the chair out of the way and bent down to pick it up, and that was when she saw something taped under the bottom of the desk.

It was another old pink manilla folder, the same as the empty one in the locked drawer.

"Well, well… weren't you a crafty old fox…" she whispered to herself with a smile. "Sal?"

Sal looked up.

"What? Have you found the rest of the letter?"

Penelope pulled the chair out of the way and, reaching under the desk, gently pulled off the duct tape that held the folder in place. With a look of triumph, she held up the folder for Sal to see.

"You're kidding me," he stammered, jumping to his feet.

"I never kid," said Penelope, placing the folder on the desk and peeling off the rest of the duct tape from the back.

She opened the folder, and both of them stared at the contents, amazed.

"What the hell do you think *that* is…" breathed Sal, his eyes widening.

Inside the old cardboard file there were two color photographs. One was a copy of the one found in his pocket of the men standing in the forest. The other was a photograph of what looked like a small strip of what was probably dark green jade, covered with tiny symbols neither of them recognized and which looked like they had been scratched or carved on it with a sharp tool. On the sides and bottom of the item were two rulers that showed the length and width, eight inches high by three across.

"That, I think…" said Penelope, "is something you might kill for."

Chapter Six

Kata

Even though the art of *iaido* had over a hundred different exercises, or *kata* as they are called in Japanese, in his daily practice periods, early in the morning when no one else was at the *dojo*, Keiichi would limit himself only to the twelve foundational exercises of the art of the sword.

To achieve these with perfect form meant that all the others would follow flawlessly, and so he began each and every day with this series of exercises, conducted seamlessly, one after the other, over and over, with complete concentration.

Each morning he would rise before dawn and take a cold shower, even in the winter months, then dress carefully in his black *iaido dogi,* pick up the small backpack and his practice sword in its black nylon case and make his way down the street to the *dojo*, where he had been trusted with his own key.

He liked this time of day the best, when he could be alone with his art with no one watching him and when he could concentrate to the limit of his ability in his lonely quest for perfection.

Ignoring the cold of the polished wooden floor, he would, at first, sit quietly in meditation for some minutes, his sword in his belt and his hands folded, left under right in his lap in the formal *seiza* position.

And then he would begin, as always, with the first *kata*, called simply *mae*, which meant 'front.'

In the art of *iaido*, there are no matches against other opponents as in the other martial arts, such as in the very closely associated art of *kendo*, where matches were fought using bamboo swords known as *shinai*. In *iaido*, there were only kata, exercises conducted alone against an imagined opponent. Nevertheless, it was regarded as *the* fundamental art of combat with the sword, and the *iaido* practitioner used a real *katana*, or Japanese sword. And in *iaido*, importantly, the imagined opponent always attacked first, thus making the art purely defensive.

During *mae*, the first of the standard twelve, it is presumed that the seated practitioner is being attacked from the front by an opponent seated directly opposite. In response, the blade is taken directly from the sheath in the belt and slashed laterally across the imagined opponent's temples in one lightning-fast movement. The *iaidoka* (or *iaido* practitioner) then rises to his feet, brings the blade above his head in another fluid motion, and then down in a direct strike to the middle of the opponent's head. He then steps back, raising the blade again and bringing it down diagonally in a motion called *chiburi*, a movement done to shake the blood from the sword, and then the sword is ever so slowly sheathed again, and the practitioner resumes his original kneeling position.

For an *iaido* master, the first three actions, the lateral slash, the frontal slash, and the *chiburi*, would probably take less than four seconds. It was meant as an explosion of power and precision that aimed at killing the opponent literally before he had time to breathe, and even though these exercises were concise, it was said that just the standard twelve *kata* took a lifetime to master.

By the time Keiichi had completed his first set of twelve and was onto the fourth *kata* of the second set, called *tsuka-ate,* the sweat was pouring off his body, and his *dogi* was soaked. In *tsuka-ate*, which meant 'to strike with the handle,' it was assumed that one was simultaneously attacked from the front and the rear by seated opponents. Using the butt of the handle as he brought out the sword from its sheath Keiichi struck the imagined opponent in front of him and now, with the sword unsheathed, whipped it directly backward to kill the opponent behind him. He then leapt to his feet and immediately brought it down on the opponent in front. Another rapid *chiburi* motion to shake off the imagined blood, another slow re-sheathing of his sword, and then once again lowering himself in a perfectly controlled manner back to his kneeling position. A slight pause to regroup, and he would rise to begin the fifth *kata*, this time a standing exercise called *kesa giri*.

One after the other, Keiichi progressed through the *kata* until the set of twelve was completed, ignoring the sweat streaming into his eyes and soaking his clothes, ignoring the screaming pain in his arms and legs as his superbly muscular body maintained a practiced and near perfect control of the most minute actions.

After he had completed several sets, he would take a break to bring his breathing back to a normal rate again, and to take stock of any errors he had noticed. This morning he was concerned with his footwork, and saw that he had repeatedly stepped back a couple of centimeters too far in the *chiburi* action. This was disturbing to him, as his master, his father, had pointed out this minor flaw before, so he stood once more and practiced the act of stepping back repeatedly until he was satisfied.

His morning practice had taken an hour, and it was now 6 a.m. The sun was peeking over the top of the neighboring buildings, and a long shaft of light was reaching through the brilliantly white paper *shoji* windows and across the floor of the *dojo* towards where he knelt, quiet now in meditation, his breathing and heart rate once again slow and steady.

He stood and packed away his sword, a beautiful practice instrument called a *tenryu,* which had a blunt edge, unlike the sharp *shinken* used in other exercises. He then carefully mopped the polished wood floor with some old towels in order to leave the place as spotless as when he found it, something that was expected of every student, no matter their rank. He took another towel from his backpack, mopped his face and his closely shaven head, and, kneeling once more, drank a liter of cold tea from a plastic bottle he had brought with him. After his strenuous workout, the tea tasted absolutely delicious, as something only can when the body craves it. He found the dehydration he suffered during his practice added to his concentration, so he never ate or drank before a session, enjoying the pain of this discipline and his victory over it.

He looked around his beloved *dojo*, a place he had been coming to since he was a little child and where his father and uncle were both masters, as he himself hoped to be one day. This was his spiritual home and his heritage, and he was proud of both.

After another cold shower at home, he had the traditional breakfast of rice, miso soup, and salmon with his mother, who was always up when he got home from the *dojo* with his food ready on the table. They never spoke very much, and he focused on eating slowly and deliberately, as to give in to the now ravenous hunger he felt and bolt down his food would be both impolite to her and an intolerable sign of weakness.

After he had eaten and washed his bowls and chopsticks, he re-packed his backpack with his books and a small notebook computer, picked up the *bento* lunchbox his mother had prepared for him, wrapped in the usual traditional blue *furoshiki* cloth, and headed out the door to his classes at the university, which was only a short train ride away and where he was studying Japanese literature, history and philosophy and was, of course, first in his class.

On his way out, he met his father, and stepping back out of his way; he made a low bow, which his father acknowledged with a mere nod.

"*Kyo, jigyu?*" Classes today? Asked his father, a tall, broad-shouldered man in his mid to late fifties who radiated power and strength, at least to his son.

"*Hai, oto-sama.*" Yes, honored father, he replied, without shifting his eyes from the ground before him. The other children used to make fun of him for using such an honorific as *sama* instead of the more common '*san*' with his own father, but in a family such as he came from, to address one's elders in any less a manner would have been an unpardonable breach of etiquette.

His father nodded and went inside, and his son quietly closed the front door and headed down the street toward the station.

That day his classes finished in the early afternoon, and so he had plenty of time to make it to his appointment at the ancient Kanda-Myojin shrine, where he was awaited by a small cadre of his friends from the university *kendo* club, some of whom also trained at his family's *dojo*.

They had chosen to meet at Kanda-Myojin not only because it was hard by Meiji university, which they all attended in Tokyo's well-known Ochanomizu district, but also because of the shrine's ancient connections to the samurai warrior class. One of the oldest shrines in Tokyo, dating back well over twelve hundred years, it was a place where the first and most important of the Tokugawa *shogun*, Tokugawa Ieyasu, the man who had finally unified Japan after centuries of civil war in 1603, had come to pay his respects to the gods for his victory.

As they gathered in the shrine's stately stone-flagged forecourt in front of the *honden,* or main hall, all of them were in a somber mood.

Hiroto Takanawa, a senior student in his final year and the oldest of the group, was the first to step forward and bow to Keiichi as he arrived.

"My condolences, Odawara," he said simply.

Keiichi bowed in return. "Thank you," he replied, as the others also stepped up and said the same thing.

Ren Minato, perhaps Keiichi's closest friend and whom he had known since his kindergarten days, was the last and did so with a tear in his eyes, which he hastily brushed away before his companions noticed. He had also been close to

Hisafumi, and his sacrifice had hit him the hardest of the group.

"Hisafumi was a hero, Keiichi-san. We are all proud of him," he said, and bowed again.

The others all murmured their agreement, and they went to sit on the front steps of the shrine as they usually did, a little away from where the small groups of worshippers were coming in to pray.

"Is there any news?" asked Takanawa, leaning forward and clasping his knees.

Keiichi shook his head.

"My aunt goes to the hospital every day, but they won't let her in. He's under police guard until he recovers, and then he'll be put on trial. Knowing him, though, there won't be a trial. He'll do what's necessary before that, I'm sure."

The others nodded their agreement.

The slayer of the impious Professor Suzuki, the profaner of the sacred imperial resting places and a piece of human filth, as far as these men were concerned, was Keiichi's cousin, and up until his arrest had been a respected member of their group and a senior student with Takanawa at the university. It was also taken as a given that even though his initial attempt at *seppuku,* or ritual suicide, had so unfortunately failed, he would no doubt avail himself of the first possible opportunity to finish the job. Death, of course, was the only way to retain one's honor when one fell into the enemy's hands.

"He'll do it without fail, we all know this," said Takanawa, who had been the only member of their group that Hisafumi had allowed to observe his final act at the theatre in Hassei university. He looked around at the others, all of whom were his sworn brothers and whom he knew were also awaiting their deaths.

"It was... beautiful. A beautiful act of destruction. I have to confess, I have never been so moved as the moment when he struck. He was like a lightning bolt, Odawara," he said calmly, clapping Keiichi on the shoulder.

Keiichi bowed his head and stared at the ground. "All of my family are proud of him," he said quietly.

Ren also put his hand on Keiichi's shoulder, and this time a tear ran down his cheek.

"We are all proud of him, Keiichi. All of us...."

Hisafumi, one of the most talented swordsmen in the group and someone who had never faltered in his commitment to the ultimate goal of the restoration of imperial rule in Japan, had volunteered for the mission to rid the world of the blaspheming professor, and the rest of the group had sworn to cut down his remaining associates as soon as they could be identified. But there was no doubt that, through Hisafumi's brave and unselfish act, they had cut off the head of the snake. The rest would now fear for their lives should they even think of tampering with an imperial tomb.

"Nevertheless," said Shota Kanagawa, a philosophy student who often attended classes with Keiichi, "We all need to watch it now. Your family, too, Keiichi. The police know who he is, and they've been at the university asking questions."

Keiichi nodded.

"They've already talked to my uncle and father as well. Of course, they told them to get lost, which of course, they did.

But they'll be back, we all know that. And my father tells me that they'll be watching the *dojo* and all the students there from this point on. This is just the beginning...."

"Keiichi is right," said Takanawa. "From now on, we must be doubly careful. Follow the rules to the letter. No communication with others on the internet, except by our usual encrypted app, and if you do that, only use the approved codenames and codewords. Only use the app in emergencies. Public phone booths or postal mail is best, and of course, burn or delete everything once you have read it. I suggest that for the next month or so we keep a low profile. Does everyone agree?"

There was another nodding of heads, and as if on cue, the group dispersed, each of them going in a different direction to avoid being followed.

Keiichi took a longer route home than usual that day, taking one train in the direction away from his house and exiting it just as the doors closed to throw off anyone who might be following him, and then taking another in a different direction, again entering just as the doors were closing. He had read about such countermeasures in spy novels and thought they sounded effective.

After taking his roundabout route, Keiichi made it to his home in the late afternoon and spent the next few hours studying before having dinner, again alone with his mother, a short docile woman who always wore kimono and loved her only son with a devotion only equaled by her fear of her husband.

After bidding her good night, he went to his room and spent an hour looking at some of the ultra-nationalist forums he was a member of, something he had been involved with since his junior high school days and where he had garnered many of his ideas.

The primary source of his views, though, had been his father and his uncle Yasuhiro, both members of Mishima's paramilitary group, the infamous Shield Society, back in the 70s, and had supported the writer's failed coup. Although they had not been asked to participate in the 'Mishima Incident,' as it came to be known on that fateful day, neither man had changed their views in the slightest. They still met with other members of the group on the anniversary of the uprising each year on November 25th, and made no secret of their views to their friends and family. Many of Keiichi's closest friends were members of the *iaido dojo* the two brothers now ran, the 'way of the sword' having been central to Mishima's reinvigorated samurai world, and all of them had grown up supporting 'the cause,' as it was known.

Of course, restoring the emperor to political power was far from being a new idea. It found its wellspring far back in the work of men such as Atsutane Hirata and Motoori Norinaga in the nineteenth century, who created educational groups advocating a return to the ancient ways where the emperor was to be revered. This movement provided the ideological basis that led to the overthrow of the shogunate that had ruled Japan for eight hundred years and the 'restoration' of the emperor to quasi-political power in 1868, and of course, the nationalist frenzy of the military period that followed.

However, even after the loss of the war and the promulgation of the new constitution, which had quashed all ideas of the emperor's divinity and even denied him the title of Head of State, the right-wing still harbored the hope of his return to power. And the most hard-core of these nationalists, who were well represented by Mishima's *tatenokai,* saw all the ills that beset Japan as rooted in the simple fact of the emperor not having the power to rule, as was his divine right.

Once restored to his rightful dignity, the 'barbarians' and their foreign culture, their clothes, food, films, and all forms of Westernization were to be rooted out and extinguished, and the purest form of Japanese culture once again established in every home. Along with this, the indigenous religion of Shinto was to be made the state religion, Buddhism and any other 'foreign' religion expelled, and democracy replaced by the absolute rule of the divine emperor, assisted by his wise courtiers. Japan would thus revert to a system of government last enjoyed during the Heian period of 1,200 years before, and the natural order of things would be restored.

For these young men, as it was for their fathers, 'the cause' was a sacred thing, and Keiichi and his friends believed themselves to be the new generation of shock troops who would bring this glorious revolution about, firstly by spilling the blood of traitors, and lastly by spilling their own. Each of them dreamt of the most exquisite of deaths, the act of ritual disembowelment, or *seppuku,* after they had accomplished the tasks asked of them by their seniors.

Before he went to bed and set his alarm, after a long discussion with an elderly man on one of the forums as to the 'filth' that was talked about in the Japanese parliament about supporting gay marriage, Keiichi laid out a fresh *dogi* for his morning practice, packed his rucksack with the other things he would need, and turned out the light.

That night he dreamed of a girl in his class at university. She had long black hair and a wonderful smile, and they often talked in the café with other friends over lunch. He dreamt of taking her, kissing her sweetly, and holding her in his strong arms one last time before leaving her on his final mission, knowing he would take his life.

Chapter Seven

The Cedars of Haguro

Penelope had been to the Tohoku region once many years before on a ski trip when she had been asked to assist in chaperoning a group of students from Hassei university's mountaineering club. It had involved a long road trip on the overnight bus from Tokyo, which was the usual way university students went skiing in the winter, as the famously uncomfortable 'night bus' was the cheapest way to get to the mountains or anywhere else in Japan, and the accommodation had been pretty spartan, to say the least.

This time however, she and Sal had opted for the far more comfortable newly opened Niigata *shinkansen*, or bullet train, which could get to Niigata, on the northwest coast of the island of Honshu, in just over two hours.

As Penelope loved trains, and particularly the bullet train, it did not take too much persuading from Sal for her to make the trip with him to the little seaside city of Tsuruoka, a couple of hours north of Niigata by local train. Fei had also said she would like to come along to make the journey even more enjoyable, and the two women had rendezvoused with Sal early one morning at Kamakura station.

The reason for the trip was rather a long shot, however.

After finding the photograph of the jade artifact hidden under his late uncle's desk, they hit a solid dead end due to the fact that whatever was written on the amulet was unreadable. Penelope, however, had seen things like it before, and guessed it was a form of proto-*kanji*, the precursor to modern Chinese characters. If so, it meant that the jade was probably from the second century BC or earlier, indicating it was an artifact from the earliest times in Japanese history, presuming it was even from Japan in the first place.

As they had absolutely no idea what it said, or even if it was a language, Penelope had made some discreet inquiries, and a copy of the photograph had been sent to an old friend of hers who was a professor of Japanese linguistics at Osaka university. Penelope and Enrico Monti, an Italian ex-pat who specialized in ancient writing systems, had once partnered on a book about Heian poetry many years previously, and she knew the now elderly professor could be trusted not to say anything if asked.

They planned to make a trip down to Osaka on the way home to see what the professor had hopefully discovered, but first Sal had other ideas, the main one being to visit the site of his uncle's murder, the tiny Choji temple on Mount Haguro, that was located just to the west of Tsuruoka, so that he could see the site for himself and talk to the head priest, who had volunteered to meet them and show them around. The other reason was that there was a slim possibility that if his uncle had taken the jade with him, then it might still be somewhere there, where he had died. Where that might be, though, was a complete mystery.

Fei had different plans as well. As a coroner, she was fascinated to see the mummified *sokushinbutsu* kept at Choji, and surprised both Penelope and Sal with the depth of her knowledge on the subject.

"It's actually something I came across when I was a student at medical college," she said as they sped on their way to Niigata on the bullet train, the dark green rice fields and little towns flashing past the big windows of the train.

"You studied how people mummified themselves? In medical school?" asked Sal, amused.

"Yeah, strangely enough… it came up. There have been a number of bodies, both ancient and modern, that have been found mummified. Not so much in Japan, the climate is too humid so the flesh rots, but in a lot of other countries. It was quite a common practice in the mountains of Peru, for example. But *sokushinbutsu*, people who mummified themselves without assistance, that's extremely rare. As far as I know, it's only been successfully done here in Japan, and it took over two hundred years of trying before the first case of it actually succeeding was recorded. I think over the nearly one thousand years people tried to do it, there were less than two dozen verified cases."

"Well, I'm glad they knocked it on the head," said Penelope. "It's barbaric if you ask me."

Fei nodded. "Yes, that's what the Meiji government said at the end of the nineteenth century. A barbaric custom that belonged to the past, they called it. But I dunno…." Fei stared out the window, and they were all silent for a while as the great dark-blue shape of Mt. Fuji reared gracefully into the sky on the left-hand side of their carriage.

"If you want to end your life, I think it should be up to you, not the government. And for those monks, they believed they were going to enter a state of permanent meditation. For them, it was a beautiful thing, and a final achievement. I think that's a personal decision."

Penelope agreed. "I haven't thought of it that way before. You may be right..." she said.

"In my job, you know, I see a lot of death. Not all of it is sad. Sometimes... it's just time to go."

"I guess so," said Sal. "So, what makes for a successful mummy, then?"

"A lot of things actually, but principally it's the diet, believe it or not," said Fei. "The *sokushinbutsu* first went on an extremely rigorous diet for three years before they died where they were only allowed to eat what they could find in the forest, which meant like nuts, buds, roots, berries, and often tree bark, which gave this diet the name of 'tree-eating.' When they were not foraging for something to eat, they were meditating on the mountain. The whole idea was to strip the body of fat, muscle, and eventually moisture, as they stopped drinking as well, in order to stop the body from decaying after death. And some of them even drank a tea made from the tree used to make Japanese lacquer. Very, very poisonous, but would have helped make the body even less available to the normal bacteria and parasites."

"They lacquered their own insides?"

Fei smiled. "In essence... yes. That's exactly what they did."

Penelope shook her head. "Wow..."

After a pleasant night's stay at one of Tsuruoka's better hot spring resorts, where they soaked away the strain and tiredness of travel and enjoyed an excellent seafood meal, they picked up their rental car the next morning and arrived at the home of the head priest of Choji temple just after breakfast.

The village of Shimaoka, nestled at the foot of Mt. Haguro, was a tiny affair, just a single street that weaved between the rice paddies with a few dozen old wooden homes on either side and not a single shop or any other facility to be seen.

They knocked on the door, and Nakanishi-san and his wife welcomed them inside, where they gathered around his huge *kotatsu* table in the spacious living room to enjoy a cup of green tea before he took them up to the temple. They were most intrigued to see Penelope, a foreigner who spoke perfect Japanese in their midst, as people like her were rare in these parts. Even as recently as when she had arrived in Japan in the early 1990s, people in this remote part of eastern Japan had probably lived their entire lives without ever laying eyes on someone from another country.

Nakanishi and his wife both gave their condolences to Sal on the death of his uncle and told him how astonished everyone had been when the body had been discovered.

"To tell the truth," said Nakanishi, "when the police chief came up here, he told me there hadn't been a murder in our district for nearly seventy years! So, you can imagine how surprised we all were...."

"Yes, thank you," replied Sal. "Our family was pretty surprised too, although having been such a long time, we were all pretty sure he was dead. It was just good to put him to rest finally."

"That's only natural," said Mrs. Nakanishi, a matronly, silver-haired woman in her early seventies, who came in to serve them some refreshments.

"This tea is wonderful, by the way," Fei remarked.

"Yes, we grow it ourselves. We don't need too much, just a few bushes for the family. Around here, that's pretty common," she said.

"That's pretty impressive, too…" said Penelope, pointing to the suit of armor in the alcove with a set of swords placed before it on an elegant lacquer rack.

Nakanishi smiled. "Yes… that's from my wife's family. Her parents only had daughters, so we ended up with it. My family has always been priests, not samurai. But it's a nice old piece, from the early 1600s, I think."

His wife nodded. "Yes, it's been in my family forever, and it's a nightmare to keep clean too. Our son comes in once a year to look after the swords, as they need to be oiled and all that, I don't know."

They finished their tea and cakes and Nakanishi drove them the short distance to a small car park where the old trail to the temple began, and they began the long climb up through a beautiful forest of cedars and pines to the temple.

"How old is this place?" said Sal, as they paused for a drink of clear spring water from an old well about halfway up.

"Choji? It's been here in one form or another since the early seventh century. The three mountains here, Gassan, Yudono, and this one, are sacred. We have a lot of *yamabushi,* Buddhist ascetic groups, coming up here regularly, so they keep us pretty busy. My family has been attending to them for centuries. And, of course, we have Entetsu Shonin, as I am sure you know. That's the main reason for people coming to Choji these days. He's one of the few *sokushinbutsu*, so we are very proud of him."

"When did he um… I don't want to say die, but…" asked Penelope.

The old priest smiled at her.

"Yes, we don't really think of *sokushinbutsu* as dead… just eternally meditating. He's been here since around 1620, so over four hundred years now. If we get a move on now, you can see him for yourself."

They reluctantly picked up their rucksacks and headed up the trail again, and in another fifteen minutes, they were at the bottom of a massive stone staircase with old stone lanterns on either side leading up to the temple.

"Oh my God," said Fei, already breathless. "How many steps are there?"

Nakanishi, who looked as fresh as a daisy, even though he was in his late 70s, looked up the staircase like he'd never noticed it before.

"Oh… I don't know. A couple of hundred, I expect… but take your time. We're all mountain people here and used to it," he said, and without another word took up his staff and began to march up the stairs like he was on flat ground.

When they finally got their breath back at the top of the staircase, they stood looking at the panoramic view of the Tohoku region that spread out before them and then entered the old temple, which the priest had now opened up for them to inspect.

"Well," said Nakanishi. "Here we are, and here is Entetsu Shonin," he gestured towards the glass case on the raised dais. "He's sort of the guardian of the temple now. This place has burned down several times over the centuries, but not once since he's been here," he said proudly.

Penelope and Fei approached the dais and looked into the eyes of the ancient monk, deep in eternal meditation amid the silence of the cedars of Mt. Haguro. The skin stretched taut across his face was a deep brown, almost black, and looked like a leather mask, but there were still bushy white eyebrows and lashes on the eyes.

"Remarkable," breathed Fei, her wonder getting the better of her professional instincts. "He really does look like he is meditating.... I've seen a lot of corpses, but nothing like this at his age."

With the priest's permission, Sal came forward and took several photos.

"So, my uncle..." began Sal.

The priest nodded that he understood and led them behind the dais to show them where his uncle's body had been found under the stage.

Sal bent down, stared into the dark hole under the dais, and shook his head.

"Wow... so sad. What a place to end up...."

The priest offered him a flashlight, and he shone the light into the dark opening.

"Was anything else found under here?" he asked.

The older man shook his head. "No, nothing, I'm afraid. He was in here all by himself. The police searched the area pretty carefully, and they had a forensics team here too... I think that's what you people call them?" he said, looking at Fei, who had joined them.

"Yep. That's what they are. They are pretty thorough. If they didn't find anything, there is probably nothing here to find," she said.

"How did he get into the temple? Is it only you with a key?" asked Penelope.

"Yes," said Nakanishi. "We have the only key. Around the time they say your uncle died, though, and it's only approximate, we did have a window in the rear smashed once. We don't know what did it, nor was there anything taken, but we assume that's how and when they got in. There were a few things knocked over inside, but that was it. It was about twenty years back, so it seems to fit."

Sal passed him back the flashlight, and they stood up and returned to the main hall.

"So, how often do people come here?" asked Penelope.

"Oh, that depends a little on the season. Not so many in the winter, except we have the odd service here for the *yamabushi* pilgrims. So during that time, there can be a few months when we don't open up. In the summer, we often have people up here, I would say at least once a week. Then we open the temple."

"So, if he was killed in the winter, it might have been some time before anyone was in here again," she added.

"Yes, and we have a problem with rats, foxes, and other animals crawling under the temple and dying. That's probably why no one noticed anything too odd as far as smells go. Like I said, we were all shocked when we found him. No one had any idea."

Penelope nodded. "What about Entetsu Shonin? Is he ever moved?"

"Yes, we move him every Year of the Ox, which is every twelve years, as you probably know. This year is the year, in fact."

"What do you do? Is there some kind of ceremony?" asked Sal.

"Yes, that's right. It's called the Ceremony of the Robes. We move the glass box from the dais, open it up and change his robes. The old robes are then cut up into tiny pieces, and we put them in these little amulet bags and sell them to people for protection and good luck. A lot of people come here for that ceremony, actually. And we sell several hundred amulets as well, which helps us keep afloat."

"I guess you have a lot of problems with the upkeep?"

"That's the biggest problem. The roof especially. It's all wood here, of course, and lots of it's rotting, so we are continually fixing things. That last earthquake, as you can see…" he pointed at the large cracks in the central pillar.

"I see your point," said Sal, running his hand along one of the cracks in the pillar.

Penelope looked up at the robed figure on the dais.

"I've just got a question," she said. "Do you change all the robes? I mean, I see a pair of shoes there in front of him? And the undergarments?"

Nakanishi looked confused.

"The shoes? No, we leave those as they are. They are just for decoration. And no, we don't touch the undergarments, just the outer robes. We wouldn't want to strip the old gentlemen in public, you know," he smiled.

"What about the cushion he's sitting on? Is that changed?"

"The cushion? No, that's not moved either, usually. We just move him."

"So, the cushion never gets moved? Ever?" she persisted.

The old priest looked at the ceiling as if trying to remember. "Well, I guess if the cushion looked like it needed replacing… but so far, it seems fine. It's never been changed since I've been priest, at least, and that's been, well… forty years or so. When I took over from my father. He was getting too old to climb up here, and had arthritis in the knees… He may have changed it, though… I don't really know."

Sal, who knew Penelope well, sensed she was on to something.

"Where are you going with this, Penny-*sensei*?"

Penelope crossed her arms and remained staring at the mummified monk.

"Tell me, Nakanishi san. Is that glass box locked?"

"Locked? No. It's just to protect our treasure there. Make sure rats don't get in, that kind of thing."

Fei gave Penelope an odd look, but said nothing.

Penelope turned to the priest.

"I know this may seem very rude, Nakanishi-san, but would it be possible to open the box so I could see inside?"

"Open it? Well…" Nakanishi looked a bit flustered. "Well… we don't usually do that… even the police didn't… well…"

Penelope remained silent and stared at the old priest with a gentle smile.

"Just for a minute? Like you said, the police never looked inside, did they? And Fei-san here does work for them…."

Fei shot her a glance but again remained silent. She was a coroner, and while she worked for the police department, she was not an actual police officer, so while what Penelope had said was true, it was a bit misleading.

It seemed to have the desired effect, though, and Nakanishi nodded.

"Well… I suppose so then… what do you want to see?"

"I'll know it when I see it, I think. May we?" said Penelope, gesturing to the glass case.

Nakanishi gave a small sigh and escorted them round to the side of the dais and up a few steps leading to the case. There was a small latch on each side which would allow them to remove the top and lower the sides to provide easy access to the figure seated inside.

The priest opened one side of the glass case and stepped back.

"Is that enough?" he asked.

Penelope stepped forward and knelt next to the glass case.

"Yes. That will be lovely, thank you. I just want to check something."

She leaned inside, and they watched as she slid her hand under the cushion where the monk sat, slowly moving her hand around.

She turned to Sal and said quietly, "I think maybe this is what we were looking for."

She slowly withdrew her hand from the box and held up a small bar of dark green jade marked with rows of tiny figures.

Sal took it from her with trembling hands, and Nakanishi and Fei crowded around him to see what she had found.

"Well, I'll be damned," whispered the old priest, astonished.

Chapter 8

The Ship to the East.

Two days later, they arrived in Osaka.

Penelope had been using her academic network to reconnect with an old acquaintance of hers, Professor Enrico Monti, a retired international scholar and a professor of the history of linguistics who used to work at Osaka University's Mino campus. Like her, he had lived in Japan for many years and, as his children were also settled here, had decided to stay rather than return to Italy for his autumn years. He also continued to write and publish on ancient writing systems, a field in which he was considered a world authority. He and Penelope had met several times in the past, mainly at academic conferences on ancient Japanese literature, and once she had even had dinner at his house with his family when she had been visiting Osaka.

He and his wife Keiko lived in a rambling, one-hundred-and-fifty-year-old former samurai residence that the professor had lovingly restored over many years in the northern Osaka suburb of Toyonaka. Most of the land belonging to the estate had been sold off long ago and turned into yet another housing estate, as it had been far too much work for the former owners to maintain, but the old mansion still survived. Now that their children had left, they lived in it alone and maintained a beautiful but manageable courtyard garden and far more rooms than they could ever use.

Professor Monti escorted his guests into one of the largest of these, his library and study, which he had constructed by removing a couple of the walls of the adjoining rooms to create a space large enough for his thousands of books and files.

"Wow…" said Penelope looking around enviously. "What I wouldn't give for a room this big. I never saw this room the last time I was here."

"Well," said Monti, "I imagine we both had the same problem when we retired. My wife was dreading it, actually. I'm sure the main thing she was dreading was having me around all the time, but more it was seeing the truck pull up with a lifetime's worth of books and stuff from my old offices at the university. So, we had to do a bit of construction work."

"Well, at least you had the room," said Penelope.

The elderly professor smiled and pointed the ladies to the sofa in front of his desk while gesturing to a large leather armchair for Sal.

"*Professoressa*," he said to Penelope, "there are rooms in this house that I don't think I have been into in ten years myself. I'm afraid to open the door and see what the mold has done. And, believe me, my dear Penelope, you would not want to be in this room in winter. No matter what you do, there is always a draft whistling between these old *shoji* and *fusuma* doors," he pointed at the white paper windows. "And in summer, my God, it is like an oven. And don't get me started on how much it would cost to replace the roof, which various tradesmen reliably tell me will collapse at the next strong earthquake... it is, in short, what you English call a 'death trap.'"

"Well, at least it's a comfortable death trap, Professor," said Fei. "I wouldn't mind it. I live with my old aunt, and I would love to put a few more rooms distance between us."

"Ah yes, there is that, *dottoressa*... a blessing when the grandchildren arrive with their hide and seek and their other loud games, that's for sure."

His wife Keiko, an elegant silver-haired lady who looked twenty years younger than her age, appeared with some tea and cakes, and after she had seen to the comfort of her guests, informed them she had to go to the supermarket, so she would leave them to her husband's mercies.

"She's gone to get things for lunch, so you must stay for that...." said the professor. "And now..." he said, reaching for a folder on his desk before they could say anything to the contrary, "let's talk about *this*."

He opened the file containing the photograph of the jade that Penny had sent him.

"I'm so glad you had a chance to look at it, Enrico. It's a bit of a mystery...."

The professor sat back in his old leather chair and smiled broadly at her. He brushed his hands through his mane of white hair and rubbed his grizzled beard, but he looked like a small child that had just been given an early Christmas present.

"Not at all, it's one of the most intriguing things I have ever seen, actually. Mystery? I would say it is a great deal more than that. Where on earth did you find it, though? I'd love to know more about its provenance… I'm sure you knew I was going to ask you about that…" he said with a wry look.

"Do you have any idea what it says?" said Penelope, sidestepping the question for the moment.

"Hmmm… that's not so easy…" he said, folding his arms across his portly chest. "As you said, it seems to be a type of proto-*kanji*, an early form of the Japanese or Chinese writing system. As such, it can be one of two things, a set of runic ideographs such as were found on tortoise shells and bones in China and used for oracular work, you know, fortune telling and so forth, and that would mean it's not saying anything specific. Or… it could be text."

"That's even more mysterious, Enrico," said Penelope looking disappointed. "What do you think it is?"

The older man shrugged. "I would say it is almost certainly text, which would date it later than anything used for shamanistic purposes, especially as it was written on what looks almost certainly like jade. I would also hazard a guess that it is also part of a story of some kind. It's very hard to say, but I was able to make out what I think are early forms of the *kanji* for 'king,' 'ship,' and 'to the East.' Of course, the old characters for 'jade' can also mean 'king,' and as I said, this looks like it was written on jade to me. If I'm right, it would almost definitely be connected in some way with royalty or the upper classes… someone important. That's where I would put my money anyway."

"Royalty? You mean Japanese royalty?" asked Penelope.

Monti threw his hands in the air in a gesture of uncertainty. "It could be. It could also be Chinese or even

Korean. It could be an imported item; as you know, there was a fair bit of trade with the continent. It depends on where it was found, really. And what or who it was found with."

"What about a date? Would you be willing to hazard a guess?" asked Sal, leaning forward in his chair.

"Oh...." said the professor with a smile. "Now you're tempting fate. If we had the original, maybe we could tell… but with just this…" he held the photograph in the air, "It could be anything from fourth century BC to 1000 BC. And like I said, it could be Chinese or Korean; as you know, the writing systems were common."

His three guests all exchanged glances, and Monti looked at them with curiosity.

"You don't mean you have it with you? The original jade?" he said excitedly.

Penelope reached into her bag and handed him a small cardboard box. Monti jumped out of his seat and hurriedly removed the lid to reveal the little jade bar they had recovered from the temple on Mt. Haguro, nestled safely between two small piles of protective cotton wool.

"Mary Mother of God," breathed the old professor, lowering the box reverently to his desk. He reached into a drawer and took out a pair of white gloves and a large magnifying glass.

"Extraordinary," he said in an awed voice. He reached into the box, turned the jade over and over, and looked at the tiny ideographs running in vertical lines on all four sides for the first time.

Finally, he put down the magnifying glass and looked at them.

"Where was this found? Do you know? Please don't tell me you came across this in a shop or someone's house…" he said in an imploring voice.

Penelope looked at Sal and nodded.

"My uncle found it."

"And your uncle was…?" asked Monti.

"He was an archaeologist and historian, a professor at Keio University in Tokyo. He died a long time ago, and he had this with him at the time."

"I'm sorry for your loss, young man. But do you know where he acquired it?" pressed Monti.

Penelope raised her hand like a student in one of his classes.

"Enrico, we are not sure exactly where it came from, but like I said when I sent you the photograph, this whole thing is highly confidential. We must know that this goes no further than this room at the moment…."

Monti smiled at her.

"Penelope… I promise you, on my life, I will tell no one. But you have to tell me. Where is this from?"

There was silence for a moment while the three guests exchanged glances and decided that they had indeed come to someone they could trust.

"Professor," said Sal. "As far as we know…we believe it came from one of the Japanese royal tombs."

The professor sat back in his chair with an air of disbelief. "Young man, that's not possible. No one has ever been allowed to access those places. And God knows we have tried to persuade them for years. You should know that."

Sal nodded.

"We do know that. Nevertheless… that's where we think it's from. And further, the people who have been connected with it, and with my uncle, have all died. And not natural deaths either…."

Monti's eyebrows shot up.

"Dead?"

"Murdered," said Sal, matter-of-factly.

A shadow seemed to fall across the room, and Monti looked down at the little jade bar and back at them, nodding to himself.

"I have heard stories… that there are powerful people here in Japan, in politics particularly, that are strongly against the opening of the royal tombs for research. We've never been able to fully understand the reason or get a decent explanation and believe me, we have tried over many years. It cannot just be, as they have said, that they regard opening the tombs as merely a profane act against the imperial family. We have always thought, particularly the archaeological and historical community, that there was more to it than just that."

His three guests looked amongst themselves.

"That would seem to be the case," said Penelope. "There has definitely been interest in any work connected to this, and not of a, well…. savory nature. That's why we want to keep any information we have concerning this as quiet as possible for the time being. So…" she leaned back in her chair. "Is there anything else you can tell us? I mean, now you can see it for yourself, what do you think it is?"

Monti placed the jade carefully back in its box and stared quietly at it for a long moment.

"If this really is, as you say, from a royal tomb, then it is quite… something. I would say it is unlikely to be a single piece. That's to say, if this is text, then it could be part of a larger body of work. Now… this is going to sound a little out there, but…Penelope… are you familiar with something called the *Shiji*?"

Penelope glanced at Sal and Fei, and they all shook their heads.

"God, don't ask me," said Fei with a smile. "I just work in a morgue."

"Yes, it's a bit beyond me, too…." said Sal.

Monti nodded and looked at Penelope, who seemed lost in thought.

"Are we talking about Fujiwara no Teika?" she asked

Monti smiled. "What a good student you are, Penelope. You forget nothing…."

Penelope was thinking back to a conference they had attended many years before where they had heard a presentation by a Chinese historian who talked about something called the *Shiji*."

"It was at that conference in Shanghai, wasn't it? I can't quite remember, but maybe in the early 2000s…."

"2003. We both attended it. And the Chinese historian we listened to?"

"Is this a quiz? Xu something?"

Monti nodded. "Xu Huan. Very interesting woman. She works in Tokyo now, actually. She talked about the Teika Fragment, the document that mentions the *Shiji*."

"So, what is it?" asked Fei.

"Well, it is a bit of a long story, and I mean that literally, but there is an ancient book of Chinese history called the

Shiji, or *The Records of the Grand Historian,* as it is usually translated. It's an absolutely vast book, a record of the first twenty-four dynasties of Chinese imperial rule. It was written in the fifth century BC by the court historian Sima Qian, and covers the first two thousand five-hundred-year period from the Yellow Emperor, the legendary first emperor of China, up to the Empress Wu, the first and only female emperor of China and the ruling monarch in Sima Qian's time. So, as I said, it's a long story...."

"But what's that got to do with us?"

Penelope leaned forward and clasped her hands on her lap.

"I think I see where Enrico is going with this. He's referring to a fragment, a part of a document that was found a long time ago, attributed to the thirteenth-century courtier Fujiwara no Teika, an extremely important man in the imperial court and the most famous poet of his time. He also made copies of several very important books, including the *Tale of Genji*. Anyway, the Teika Fragment, and we know it is his because we know his calligraphy well, says that as a gift to the emperor of the time, I think that was Go-Toba?.... That he was going to dedicate himself to writing a Japanese version of the *Shiji*, and that for this purpose he would base the earliest history of the imperial line on something called the Jade Scroll, which was supposedly an ancient document written on jade that detailed the earliest history of the Japanese imperial line."

Sal sat up straight.

"Why do you say 'supposedly'?

Enrico shrugged. "Because Fujiwara's reference to the Jade Scroll is the only extant mention of its existence. And

Fujiwara never seems to have gotten around to his great project either. And the Scroll has never been found. But Fujiwara is talking about something that presumably did exist in the thirteenth century and was already regarded as clearly very ancient."

"So, what are you guys saying?" asked Fei.

Enrico and Penelope exchanged glances, and Penelope smiled at them.

"I think what we might infer is that this piece of jade…" began Monti

"Is part of the Jade Scroll?" asked Sal, his eyes widening.

Enrico leaned forward in his chair.

"It's just a supposition. It could be part of it, or it could be part of something like it. But it's an interesting idea, don't you think?

There was silence in the room for a while and Monti sipped his tea.

"But if this *is* part of the Scroll, and it's talking about a king that came over the sea to the East, isn't that talking about him coming from China to Japan? And wouldn't be that suggesting there may be another story about the imperial line?" asked Sal.

"Very perceptive, young man," said Monti. "The imperial bloodline is still taken very seriously. The business about him being divine, though, was of course a much later concoction, or rather a spurious emphasis of the nineteenth century to give credence to the restoration of imperial rule at the time… but the bloodline is a different matter. That's a serious thing and is still seen as such. Just hop onto the imperial homepage, and you can see it all spelled out right there. Teika might have been posing them a direct threat."

"I would say exposing the imperial line as having a Chinese base would qualify as such, right?" said Sal.

Penelope smiled and shrugged. "Well, Teika was on famously bad terms with the emperor, and sided with the early *shogun* Minamoto no Sanetomo. He was his poetry teacher when he was young…."

"So, his book might not have been a welcome present?" asked Fei.

Monti laughed. "Possibly not. And if Go-Toba knew about the Jade Scroll, he might have sought to destroy it….."

"Which meant Teika could have hidden it?" asked Sal.

The old professor held up his hands in a gesture of giving up.

"Now we are just playing a game of supposition, aren't we? Anyway, it was just a thought.

He again picked up the jade in his white-gloved hands and turned it over lovingly.

"Wouldn't it be interesting, though…"

Chapter 9

All the Emperor's Men

Masakichi Bando, like many people who spend their lives in politics, and even like the more controversial ones whom people heartily detested and for good reason, was not necessarily badly intentioned. Whatever others thought of him, he saw himself as an old-fashioned patriot in the image of the great revolutionary leaders of the past, and he genuinely believed that he was serving the best interests of his nation and working for its benefit. One could argue, of course, that so did Hitler and the other great arch-villains of history, and in that, you would be correct. Yet, politics is evil only in the manner of its execution, and unfortunately, like Hitler, the *kuromaku* sincerely believed that the means justified the end.

Therein lay the problem, of course.

Bando and the other unthinking ideologues that followed him, saw their politics as an act of service to a nation that really did not understand what was in their best interests. They believed that it didn't really matter *what* the general public thought, as they had been corrupted by poor education and foreign cultures and were thus ignorant and in need of guidance. Therefore, the state would act in their best interest, and do whatever was necessary for what it saw as the public good. And although it was now too late and they were too weak to do what could be considered the ultimate good, the restoration of divine imperial rule, it was still possible to guide the public in the right direction by simply disregarding what they thought and telling them that they were acting in the cause of national 'stability,' which was an argument that had been accepted over and over for generations in Japan to cover a multitude of sins.

After the vicissitudes inflicted by the war, this was seen as the one absolute necessity for public order and good government, and why the nation had vested power in the same party, with just minor divergencies, for the entire post-war period.

Born at the height of the Pacific War himself, he had grown up in an important political family, which had managed to survive and even flourish after the war, and this despite the inconvenience of his father being temporarily imprisoned as a war criminal. He had grown up thus shielded from poverty and the repercussions that had flowed from the wartime acts that people like his father had inflicted upon the people in the name of the emperor, and come to see much of what had happened at that time as an essentially correct but bungled act of aggression. If they had avoided war with the Americans, in all likelihood a deal would have been done where they would have been left with the lands they had conquered and their national dignity intact, and all for the small price of acting as a buffer against the communists and Russia, which was something Bando and his ilk had no problem with at all.

He had spent his life on a single mission, basically the same one pushed on the public during the war, of defending the country from the West. In his mind, protecting the nation from the West, and especially from the creeping vileness of its insidious 'culture,' was the primary objective today and the only way they would one day be able to restore the emperor to his divinely appointed role. If Western culture (if it could even be called that) were allowed to have free reign, then his nation would be irrevocably changed and it would only be a matter of time before the very idea of what it meant to be Japanese and even the imperial family itself, would be dropped into the dustbin of history. And as a pure-blood fascist, that was not an option he could allow.

Small though their group was, it was relatively easy to find people who agreed with them, especially as the general public still felt that respecting Japanese traditions was a kind of moral duty, and the thing that made them unique and better than the corrupt people of other countries. The more they hammered this line, the more supporters they got. At the same time, as the economy slowly worsened over the last several decades and Japan gave up its leading place in the pecking order of world economies, the more business had picked up.

But it was not all smooth sailing, and in these sad days when he had unfortunately lived long enough to see Japanese culture denoted as simply comic books, 'cosplay' and animated movies, he knew they were well and truly on the back foot when it came to having any say in popular opinion such as they had maintained in the 'good old days' of the military period, when classical Japanese culture, and especially the martial arts, had been co-opted as part of the nationalism of the times.

This evening especially, as he had his near-daily audience with his top lieutenant, the wizened and unctuous Yasunori Katayama, he felt that things were moving decidedly against them, and that firm action would need to be taken immediately.

That evening he had ordered a particularly fine bottle of *sake* from Yamaguchi prefecture, his old home, and some excellent *sashimi* he had ordered brought from the new central fish market at Toyocho that morning. Katayama, for his part, knew that it was a singular honor to be allowed to dine with the Boss, and made sure he complimented everything in sight in the appropriately subtle manner that his superior enjoyed.

"Ah, you know," he said as he downed another shot of *sake* from the elegant *bizen* ware glass he had been given, "Yamaguchi really does make some of the finest *sake*. Is this *Dassai*?" he said, knowing full well what brand it was.

"Yes," said his boss, favoring him with the briefest of smiles. "It's superb with this sea bream. Don't you think?"

Katayama smiled obsequiously.

"What a wonderful choice. I would never have thought of combining *this* fish with *this sake*," he lied. "I would have gone for something heavier. Maybe a *gin meishu*...."

"Oh no, that would never do," said Bando, waving his hand like there was a mosquito in the room. "Not with a fish like this. You need something quieter...."

Katayama nodded. "Yes, you're right. I can see that now."

There was silence between the two men for a few moments, and then Bando asked the question that Katayama had been dreading all along.

"And how are things proceeding with the Suzuki matter?" he asked without looking up.

Katayama tried to deflect talking about what had happened since the professor's killing, but he knew it was useless. In the end, he would have to tell him everything, because God alone knew what would happen to him if the Boss found out through some other source. The man had ears everywhere, and there were just too many people who would fall over themselves to curry favor with him by giving him intelligence about something which might benefit the cause in some way, or simply Bando's own welfare.

"I think it's under control… as well as can be expected," he hedged. "We're waiting….."

The older man looked up, and a wave of annoyance passed across his face.

"Waiting? Waiting for what? Has the boy been disposed of yet? Or disposed of himself?"

Katayama felt the cold breeze of fear he knew all too well in these interviews.

"Yes… well. No doubt he will take his own life at the first opportunity. We are confident of that. Yes, confident…"

Bando nodded. "And he has still not spoken to the police?"

"No. Our person in the Kamakura police has confirmed that."

"The fellow from Tokyo?"

"Yes. He's quite highly placed now. He has the confidence of the senior officer on the case… I think his name is Chief Inspector Yamashita."

"Very good. And what about this journalist? What's being done about him?"

Katayama felt the color drain out of his face.

"Yes, well, there's been a few developments on that front. This morning I received a phone call….."

He could tell that Bando was angry now, and he began to flounder, trying to find the right words to tell him that things had actually taken a decidedly nasty turn.

"A phone call from whom?"

"From er… one of our contacts. In Niigata. The er… priest."

The older man was silent for a moment as he rapidly connected the dots, and the fact that he had to do this made him even more annoyed, and also feeling like he was not being told what he needed to know. An act of betrayal. Someone would have to pay for that.

He looked steadily at Katayama like a snake watching a mouse.

"Are you talking about the priest at that temple where the body was found? The body that the person *you* assigned to dispose of so stupidly *hid* instead of doing what he had been instructed? That priest?"

Katayama looked down at the spotless tatami mats, but there was nothing there that could save him now, and he knew it.

"Yes, sir. That priest. We've been donating to his temple, you know, for the last few months since the body was discovered. And we asked him to call us if there were any developments…."

"And?"

"Apparently, the journalist Nakamura and some other people visited the temple last week."

"And why would they do that?"

"Well... as you know, Nakamura is the murdered man's nephew."

"Yes, I know all that. Why was he *there*?"

Katayama gulped.

"Well, apparently... they were looking for something... Perhaps what we have been seeking ourselves. They recently spent some time at the uncle's house, and then they went to Niigata...."

"You mean... they are looking for what was taken from the tomb? Twenty years ago? Are you telling me they know about that now?"

"Possibly... we're not sure. Remember, sir; we don't even know if something *was* taken...."

Bando looked at him like he was something found on the bottom of his shoe.

"Of course, something was taken, you clown. Why else would they have run off like that? We always thought the uncle had taken something and fled with it. That's why we had that temple searched after the murder in the first place. Unfortunately, the swine must have hidden it somewhere else. Is that all the priest said? That they were there?"

"No, sir. He said they found something. Something that had been hidden there...."

There was an icy silence in the room for a moment, and then the question came in a whispered voice that made Katayama almost soil himself.

"What did they find, you fool? And why wasn't I informed at once?"

Katayama bowed low to the floor in apology and stayed there while he spoke.

"I deeply apologize, sir. It didn't seem important. They found some stone item with something written on it. The priest had no idea what it was. I'm sorry…" he whimpered, his gaze fixed on the tatami mat.

Then there was the sound of the sake flask shattering against the wall above his head, and when he glanced up, Bando was on his feet and towering over him in a rage he had rarely seen before. A moment later, the door flew open, and one of the security staff entered with his hand on the holster of his gun.

"Whoever has this item, I want that person found. Immediately. And I want whatever it is that he has returned to me. Do you understand?" he hissed fiercely.

Katayama touched his forehead to the tatami mat.

"*Hai*!" he shouted.

Bando took a deep breath and returned to his cushion.

"Now you may leave," he said coldly.

====================

It had been a quiet trip back to Tokyo for Penelope and her friends. For some reason everyone seemed to be lost in their own thoughts, and no one felt like talking about what they had discovered. Sal had entrusted the jade to Penelope as a safety measure, and it was secure in its little box at the bottom of her rucksack, which she never let out of her sight.

A few hours after leaving Osaka, they were back home in Kamakura, and Sal parted with them at the station to return to his house and put his thoughts in order before they made any more moves.

Penelope's cats, whom she had entrusted to the care of her neighbor and tea ceremony teacher Fujiwara-san, were lined up at the front door waiting for her the moment they heard the key turn in the lock, and as usual, they had been well looked after by the ever-attentive older woman whom Penelope had known for many years.

A little later, Fei joined her again, and they spent a few hours attending to the vegetable garden and harvesting some potatoes, which Penelope planned to cook for their evening meal, which she had invited Fei to take with her that night.

As she was washing the vegetables, her phone rang, and she heard the familiar voice of Chief Inspector Yamashita on the other end of the line wanting to know if she was free to talk about something urgent.

"Why don't you come for dinner? Fei is going to be here too…" she said, knowing the inspector, an inveterate bachelor, rarely said no to a home-cooked meal.

"You're on. I'll bring the wine."

"Excellent," said Penelope with a smile.

At the appointed hour that evening, Yamashita-san appeared with an outrageously expensive bottle of Chablis that he knew Penelope liked, and the three of them sat down to eat.

"So, what's the big news?" asked Fei.

Yamashita put down his forkful of the steak Penelope had served them.

"Not good news, I'm afraid. Young Odawara has been feeling much better, apparently. He made a good recovery from his wounds and was transferred to a police infirmary to finish his convalescence before we can take him before a judge."

"Well…that's *good* news, isn't it?"

Yamashita looked at his plate.

"He killed himself the moment he got there. Hung himself with a bed sheet. Apparently, the guard hadn't been watching him as carefully as he should have. He's gone."

"Good God…." said Penelope.

"Indeed," said Yamashita. "I have no idea why the guard wasn't paying attention. They had strict instructions to watch him 24/7, especially as he was obviously a major suicide risk. But…"

"Well, it must be hard to keep up that level of surveillance, I guess…."

Yamashita cocked his head to one side and raised an eyebrow.

"Well… that's one excuse, I suppose…."

Fei leaned forward and gave him an enquiring look.

"What is it you are not telling us, Eiji-san?"

Yamashita looked at her strangely.

"What am *I* not telling you? Let me see. That's a good question… I'm really wondering what *you two* are not telling *me*. About what you were up to in Osaka? I talked to Sal earlier in the day…."

Penelope smiled and patted him on the hand.

"You first… then I promise we'll come clean, officer."

"Hmmm…" Yamashita frowned. "So, that's how it is, is it? OK, then. Let's talk about young Odawara. We've been investigating him, and I must admit he has a colorful pedigree, as you know. His father and uncle were both *tatenokai* like I told you before, and the kid himself belonged to his own dark little group which our counter-terrorist group in Tokyo has been monitoring for over a year due to their very nasty-sounding online presence and the fact they never seem to share messages lately anymore. A piece of very odd timing which has not gone unnoticed, shall we say."

"What do you mean, online presence? Chat rooms?"

"Yes, that and trolling other groups seem to have been their main leisure activity lately. They used to be pretty active up until recently, but radio silence seems to have descended a few weeks before Odawara's murder of Professor Suzuki. Further to that, it appears that all evidence of the professor's work and what he was going to be talking about has been wiped."

"Wiped? You mean it's gone?" asked Penelope.

Yamashita nodded. "Gone. All of it. Either he deleted it himself to protect it, or his university server was hacked. His laptop at the scene and any he may have had at home are also gone. We are still going through all his files, which could take years by the way, but at the moment, we are pretty much in the dark. Oh, and his main research assistant, a guy called Miyamoto, has completely disappeared."

"Wow… so you think…"

Yamashita took a sip of his wine.

"I think the police have a mole on their hands."

There was a stunned silence for a moment.

"A mole? Someone working for these right-wing groups?" asked Fei.

"Or at least sympathetic to them. Yes. I think that it is much bigger than anyone is letting on. I don't think those kids Odawara was running around with have the technical know-how to pull off a hack like that. If it *was* a hack, as I said we are not sure yet. As far as we know, none of them has expertise in that area. They are simply, how shall I put it delicately… blunt instruments."

"You mean they are thick as cheese," said Fei in English, delighting as always in showing off her knowledge of British English slang.

Yamashita laughed. "Something along those lines. It goes with the territory of being a sword-swinging right-wing nutcase. But we've also been investigating Daddy's *iaido dojo*. I'm guessing you don't know about that?"

"Only that he had one," said Penelope. "What about it?"

"Well, those places don't make much money these days, and most are small, family-run businesses. Theirs is pretty well-known in the *iaido* world, and they publish their own little magazine, both an online and a print version. They've been doing it for like thirty years or so. They kind of cottoned on to the internet quite early; it would seem. Anyway, let me show you something…."

Yamashita reached into his old leather briefcase and brought out a shiny new iPad.

"Oh… police issue?" said Fei. "They gave me one a few years ago too. The cheapest model, of course…."

Yamashita fired up the device and put it on the table so they could see.

The screen showed the front cover of a magazine with a very good color picture of someone in full *iaido* garb doing what looked like a *kata* with a beautiful, bright *katana*.

"Nice sword," said Penelope dryly.

Yamashita nodded. "No doubt they think so too. Odawara's cousin, Keiichi, who is about the same age, looks after the webpage for his elders."

"Children at least have some use," Fei sighed.

"Yes, so it would appear. Anyway, it's *this* that got our attention."

Yamashita scrolled through several pages until he found a picture featuring a group of men dressed in black *kimono* standing behind another line of younger men kneeling in front of them with their black-sheathed swords.

"And this is what?" asked Penelope, looking closely at the photograph.

"This, ladies, is graduation day, it seems. Presentation of different black-belt *dan* certificates. And this guy...." Yamashita pointed the tip of his pen at a black-clothed older man with a long thin face who looked to be in his late seventies. "This is Katayama Yasunori. An uncle by marriage of the Odawara brothers, and a generous donor to his nephew's business over the years. A *very* generous donor...."

"I see. And that makes him dodgy?" asked Fei.

"That makes him dodgy.... That and the fact that he is a former member of parliament and very well connected with a certain right-wing group in the ruling party called the *Shinenkai*. Otherwise known as the *New Flame Society*. Heard of them?"

Penelope shook her head, yet Fei, an avid consumer of political news, raised her eyebrows. "Oh yeah… them. But they have lots of members. Nothing that outrageous. You would have to lock up half the Japanese parliament if they were as nasty as Odawara."

Yamashita nodded. "That's true, and a thought that has crossed my mind more than once."

"You'll have to enlighten me further, I'm afraid. What does this group do?" asked Penelope, going to the kitchen to get another bottle of wine.

"They are a *Shinto* religious cult within the parliament, and they have some pretty high-up members, including many former and present cabinet members."

"That's true," said Fei. "They like to keep a low profile, but they are like an octopus across many of the most important factions. It's amazing how many of their members get the good jobs. Being a member is seen by many as necessary if you are going to get ahead."

"So, do they have any goals apart from just being some kind of super faction?" asked Penelope.

"That's an excellent question, Penny-*sensei*, and kind of why I am bringing them up. They do have another goal, and it is the same one as the Odawara brothers and their ultra-right friends."

"Which is? Don't be coy, Eiji." She said, giving him a sly smile.

"They want to see an absolute monarchy in Japan. They want the emperor to be head-of-state with a veto on any law made up by parliament. In short, they want to turn back the clock not just to the Meiji period of the nineteenth century, but right back to the Heian period of a thousand years ago. A full restoration of Imperial and court power."

"Wow… crazy. But that's got like zero support these days, right?"

"That's true, it's a total non-starter. But the thing I keep wondering is this. If the Odawara brothers and their nutty little group of sword enthusiasts don't have the brains to get rid of the professor's research… whom do they know who does? And how did they even know what the professor was researching? If they are the gun, who's holding it?"

He tapped his fountain pen on the picture of the grim-face Katayama in the photograph.

"Who indeed…" whispered Fei.

Chapter 10

The Singing Blade

Three days later, Sal, Penelope, and Fei were ushered into Professor Xu Huan's rather cramped office at Toyoshima university in central Tokyo, where the professor insisted on making them cups of jasmine tea in big Chinese mugs before they were allowed to talk about anything else.

Professor Xu was just as Penelope remembered her at the conference she had attended so many years before, a short woman with thick, black-framed glasses which made her eyes look rather owl-like, shoulder-length dark hair pulled back in a ponytail, and with a no-nonsense air about her. She wore a tailored black suit with a plain white blouse, and Penelope remembered that was exactly what she had worn when they had met maybe twenty years previously. She also didn't look a day older, which Penelope rather envied. The professor also reminded her a lot of Fei, whom Penelope had brought with her that day, just in case seeing another Chinese in the room might help things along. She needn't have bothered, though, as Professor Xu was completely at ease speaking with them and also, being a professional historian, fascinated by what they had to say.

"So... you are Professor Nakamura's nephew? I was very saddened to hear about his disappearance, what? It must be twenty or so years ago now?"

"Yes, that's right. His body was only just discovered recently. In Niigata."

The Professor nodded and handed him a large mug of tea with the traditional Chinese lid.

"That's so sad. May he rest in peace. I'm sure it must be a great relief for your family, though. To know what happened."

Sal nodded.

"Maybe you were unaware of this, but I knew your uncle," she said.

"You knew him?" said Sal, surprised.

"Yes. He and my father were quite close friends. My dad was also an archaeologist, with the national university in Hunan province. They worked on several papers together. I knew him quite well when I was an undergraduate. When my father was too busy, I used to accompany him, you know, as a sort of tour guide to various places. He was a very nice person." she said rather wistfully.

"What kind of things did they work on together?" asked Fei.

"Well, all kinds of things. My father was a specialist in early marine history, and Professor Nakamura was interested in early migration from the continent to the Japanese peninsula."

"So...sort of where the Japanese came from?" asked Penelope.

"Yes, that's right. And the early kingdoms in the pre-Nara period. It's something many of my students here seem to have very strange ideas about."

"How so?" asked Sal.

Professor Xu laughed and shook her head so that her hair flew about wildly, and she threw her hands in the air in a rather emphatic way that you would never see a Japanese person do, which made Penelope rather like her.

"Oh… you know. If you read Japanese middle school textbooks, the whole idea of the Japanese coming from somewhere else is rather downplayed. It's like they sprang up from the earth like the flowers, you know, all children of the Shinto gods, the pure Yamato line and all that stuff. It's like they have 'we're unique' stamped on their foreheads. When I tell them they have the same DNA as people from Kazakhstan and Central Asia, they look rather confused."

"I'll bet. I didn't know that myself, actually," said Sal.

"Nah… no one does. Anyway, please tell me all about Professor Suzuki. I knew him quite well too. It sounded horrific…" she said, becoming serious again.

Penelope recounted the story of what had happened at the conference, and when she finished Professor Xu turned, and seemed to quickly wipe away a tear.

"It's… I don't know… so unnecessary. He was a fine scholar and a lovely man. Why would anyone want to kill him? It's just… surreal somehow…." she said, trying to get a grip on her emotions.

"That's what we are trying to understand too. We've uncovered a few things that may be connected to his death… but we are not really sure of anything. That's why we came to see you," said Penelope.

"To talk about the *Shiji*? And the Teika Fragment? You're welcome, but I don't know how it all ties into Professor Suzuki's death. I gather Enrico suggested talking to me?"

Penelope smiled. "Yes, it was his idea. And mine too. I wanted to talk to you, particularly…. about the Jade Scroll."

"Ah… the Scroll," nodded Professor Xu thoughtfully. "Now… wouldn't that answer some questions! But the Teika Fragment is the only mention of it historically. Its existence has always been a mystery."

"But the Fragment indicates that it was once in Tieka no Fujiwara's possession?"

"Yes, so it says."

"And you have no reason to believe that was untrue?"

Professor Xu was silent for a moment and then tapped her pen on the desk like she had made a decision.

"No, I don't. I think if he said it, then it was true. What he said about writing some form of Japanese history based on the Scroll was meant as a direct threat to Emperor Go-Toba. That's pretty clear. And if it *was* meant as a threat, it would not have carried any weight unless the emperor was also aware of the Scroll's existence. So, I believe he had it. At least at one point."

Penelope nodded. "That's exactly what Enrico and I think as well. So… the question is this. *If* he thought the Scroll was in danger, where do you think he would have hidden it?"

Professor Xu smiled broadly and threw up her hands.

"You're guess is as good as mine. But somewhere where it would have been safe long-term. Perhaps a friendly monastery?"

"That's a possibility, I guess. Although most likely by this time, there would have been some record of it being stored."

"That's true. Unless it was destroyed at some later date. Maybe in a fire or something… that happened a lot, as you probably know."

Penelope looked at Sal, who nodded to the bag that Penelope was holding on her lap.

"Professor, would you mind having a look at something and giving us your opinion?"

The professor looked surprised. "Sure. What is it?"

Penelope passed her the cardboard box containing the little rectangle of jade, and the professor placed it carefully on her desk and removed the lid. The moment she did so, her eyes widened, and they all heard her gasp.

"Oh my God…" she said, reverently taking it in her hands and turning it over and over. She reached into a drawer, took out a large magnifying glass just as Enrico Monti had, and spent several minutes staring at the small but evenly etched inscriptions on the four sides.

"Where did you get this?" she said, looking up at them in wonder.

"That was Enrico's first question too… Can you read any of it?"

Professor Xu shook her head and sighed. "That's really much more of a question for Enrico than me. But my gut reaction is that it's text. This kanji may be 'ship'. I'm wondering if this line…" she pointed to several characters with the tip of a pen, especially to a set of four characters on the reverse side. "It may indicate a journey of some kind. To the east… that may indicate Japan. And this could be 'King'…" she said, pointing at another character. "It's amazing…" she picked up her magnifying glass again and stared at the jade for a long time.

"Do you have any idea about a date?" asked Sal.

"A date? Oh…. That's really pushing it. But proto-*kanji* like this, and the shape… I would say pre-fourth century Chinese."

"Chinese?"

"Yes. Almost definitely Chinese."

"Why do you say that?"

Professor Xu picked up her pen and traced the outline of the disc. "Because of the shape. Jade bars like this have been found before, also with text. Before paper became widespread, people wrote on bamboo strips and tied them together. Jade inscriptions like this are a bit different, however, they follow the same idea, just a lot more expensive and time-consuming to make. They were usually the property of royalty or someone of high position. Sometimes they told a story about that person, which was why we found them in tombs, you know, as funerary objects."

Penelope looked at Sal and Fei, who were both nodding in agreement.

"Well, it's strange you should say that, because we believe this also came from a tomb. A royal tomb, perhaps."

"A Chinese royal tomb? Well, I suppose that would be my guess too."

Penelope shook her head, and the Professor gave her a strange look.

"Not a Chinese tomb, professor. A Japanese one."

The professor's mouth dropped open, and she shook her head.

"You're sure of this? Which tomb? Wow… that would be a bombshell for sure…."

Penelope smiled. "I guess it would. But here is the thing I am wondering. This artifact, according to Enrico, talks about a king going to the East. I'm guessing that's from China or Korea. Either way, it's maybe part of some larger historical record…."

The professor stared at them with a shocked expression and then at the jade.

"Are you saying you think this is part of the Jade Scroll?" she asked quietly.

Penelope looked at Sal again and took out the photograph of the group of archaeologists and passed it to her.

"Wow… where did you get this? Oh… there is your uncle… and Professor Suzuki… they look so young here, don't they…."

Penelope smiled. "I guess they do. Do you have any idea where this was taken?"

Professor Xu nodded.

"Maybe I do. Or I can find out. My father knew, of course, but he's no longer with us, unfortunately…."

Penelope stared at her, astonished.

"Your father? But he is not in the picture… we know who the other men are."

Professor Xu looked up from the photo and smiled.

"Oh, I know that. He was the one taking the picture…."

====================

Shortly after the slaying of his old boss and mentor, Professor Suzuki, his main research assistant Jun Miyamoto had quietly taken an extended leave of absence for 'family reasons' from the old Kamakura university where he had worked for so many years, and headed for his grandmother's house in Nagasaki prefecture.

He hadn't really known where he should go, only that it had to be some remote, hard-to-find place where he could think about what to do and that it had to be now.

Right now.

Fortunately for Jun, and indeed for all his family, his ancestral home was the first place that came to mind whenever the words 'far away' were floated, and indeed it was exactly that.

He had arrived in the grey light of early dawn, exhausted after having driven for more than fourteen hours straight, but still unable to shake off the feeling of dread that had followed him ever since the shocking events of the week before. He hadn't dared take a bus or a plane, or even the bullet train, which would have been far quicker and much more comfortable. Instead, he had hightailed it in his old Toyota sedan, which he figured correctly he would need once he got where he was going.

His old family home in the beautiful seaside prefecture Nagasaki had been where his father had grown up, and where several other generations of his family had lived. However, after he graduated from university in Tokyo, his father decided to pursue a banking career in the capital, and Jun was born and raised in Kamakura. He, in turn, had chosen a career in archaeology at Hassei university, the largest university in the city, and one which had an impressive school headed by Professor Suzuki, who had become his mentor and almost like a second father to him.

But that was all behind him now, at least for the time being.

The house was located quite far from Nagasaki city, in the old castle town of Hirado, one of those unspoiled and atmospheric Japanese towns by the sea, and not far from the old Dutch trading post. His family had thus not been in Nagasaki city, as some of their relatives and friends had been, on that fateful day in 1945 when the atomic blast had leveled the town and killed thirty-five thousand people. Instead, they had continued to live quietly in Hirado, one of the westernmost places in Japan, and which was actually on an island joined to the mainland by a short bridge, and so generally spared the ravages of the war.

As his grandparents had died and his own parents had gotten older now, their visits to the old house had become less and less frequent, and it was only he and his sister who occasionally visited, mainly to look after the family grave, which was situated at a nearby temple on a beautiful hill of bamboo and pine looking out over the water and just a few hundred meters away from their house.

As he opened the front door, he noticed that the old maple tree just above the doorway was beginning to show the first signs of autumn. It brought back memories of the days when his grandparents were alive, and how his family had always enjoyed the splendid colors of this tree and how it had seemed like a gift just for his family, a harbinger of the much-loved New Year period which was now not far away and when all the extended family used to gather here.

It was a different story now, though.

The house smelled of mold and dank, as the summers in Nagasaki were intensely hot and punctuated by regular typhoons, which often brought devastating rains and mudslides in their wake. He knew he would have to spend at least a day cleaning and trying to make the place livable if he was going to have any semblance of comfort here.

He unloaded the car and threw his bags in the bedroom he usually slept in, and then after opening all the windows and shutters to air the rooms, he headed down to the local convenience store to pick up some supplies. On his return, he took the bedding out of the cupboards and hung them outside, as they were in pretty bad shape due to the pervasive dampness.

His plan was to stay here until at least the New Year and to use the time to figure out what to do. He had no idea what direction was the correct one, and it had been something that had been bothering him constantly since his professor's death at the hands of the young monster with his sword. Even now, revisiting the scene in his mind, the thought of it made him shudder, and he could not help replaying over and over again the moment when the man rushed at his professor after jumping onto the stage. Suzuki, a kind and gentle soul, had never stood a chance.

Kindly and helpful as he was, though, Jun also knew he was extremely astute and far from the naive version of the absent-minded academic that people may have taken him for. He had been aware of the gravity of his work, and more than aware that he had powerful enemies beginning to range themselves against him. He had thus been preparing Jun for the possibility of something bad happening for months, a fear that he had only shared with him, his closest and most senior student.

It was only now he understood why the professor had been nervous and taking precautions, yet, even so, he did not understand fully what it was that had him so spooked.

One evening, about a week before his death, the professor had summoned him to his large, book-lined office for a meeting that he now understood would change the course of his life.

It had been a quiet evening just after dinner, and he had strolled across the silent campus to the old building that housed the Department of Archaeology and History under a bright moon and the smell of the nearby ocean lingering on the breeze, which was just beginning to turn cooler as the autumn began to deepen.

The professor had been waiting for him, and had ushered him quickly into the room and given him a glass of tea. Although the professor was his boss, and the head of the Department, their relationship had deepened over the many years Jun had worked for him, ever since his undergraduate days, and now it was far more like that of father and son. He had never known why this brilliant man had taken such a liking to him, but he was more than grateful that he had. He knew quite well that without him it was very likely that his career as an academic would have amounted to very little, and he was more than happy to focus on helping his mentor achieve his far more important aims and to dedicate himself to his work.

The professor had sat behind his big desk that night, behind the usual piles of papers and books that littered it, and even though Suzuki was in an amiable and good-natured mood, Jun could see that something was weighing on the older man's mind. One of the ways he knew this was that, quite uncharacteristically for him, he had gotten straight to the point.

"I need you to do something for me, Jun-san," he said, folding his arms and puffing on his old western-style pipe, something he always did in the privacy of his room and in flagrant breach of the university's strict no-smoking policy.

Jun had leaned forward and clasped his hands before him.

"Sure, what's up?"

A grim look passed over the older man's face.

"You remember how they recently found the body of Professor Nakamura?"

Jun nodded that he did. Even though it had been a long time ago, he remembered working with Nakamura on several important digs, and he also knew the story of the professor's disappearance and something of the circumstances around it. It had been a mystery that had obviously remained a sore point for many years with his old boss, whom he knew had had a close relationship with him. He also knew that at the time of Nakamura's disappearance, they had been working together on something private, a project that they had not shared with anyone else, even him. In those years Jun had, of course, asked several times what the nature of this research had been, but his mentor had only provided the vaguest of answers in response.

Now though, he sensed the situation had changed.

"Yes, of course, terrible..." he replied, the story having been big news in their department.

"Well, there are some things I need to tell you, and I also want you to know what to do in case anything.... Well, just in case."

"What do you need, *sensei*?"

The professor sighed and handed him a small red USB flash drive.

"I need you to take this, and I need you to promise me that you will not tell anyone about it and that you will not look at it unless I or someone I appoint gives you specific instructions to do so. Are we clear?"

He gave Jun a serious look and continued.

"On this drive is all my research into a certain matter involving Professor Nakamura, myself, and several others. You will also find a copy of the presentation I am going to give, which will make that research public for the first time. I have to tell you, though, Jun-san, that this may be very serious repercussions. You need to be aware of this."

Jun sat up, shocked at what Professor Suzuki had just said. The man he knew was a model of academic probity who demanded the same from all his students. He could not imagine what he had done that would warrant such fears.

"Seriously?" he asked.

"Seriously," intoned his boss, peering at him over the top of his glasses and giving him a faint smile. "But there is more, Jun-san. Much more. Professor Nakamura was not the only one to die as a result of our research. Oh, yes, don't look surprised. That's exactly why he was killed. This research touched upon... shall we just say, a sensitive historical issue. Something that certain people, especially in the government, would rather remain not spoken of…."

He looked out the darkened window of his office, and then got up and pulled the heavy curtain closed as if to block out the night and also anyone who might be watching.

Jun examined the flash drive between his fingers and wondered what to say.

The professor resumed his seat and leaned forward with his elbows on the desk and his ever-present pipe in his hand.

"Listen to me carefully Jun-san," he began in a slightly sad tone. "As you know, even though there is a great deal of archaeological work going on in this country there are certain places, those connected with the ancient royal family especially, where we are not allowed to go. You know this as well as I, and you also know that we have petitioned the government to allow us to conduct our work, our important historical work, for many, many years. All to no avail, of course…."

He gave Jun a rueful smile and ran his hands over his short-cut silver hair. He pushed his glasses up his nose with his middle finger and stared at the younger man with his dark, intelligent eyes. Jun leaned forward despite himself and felt a slow, creeping fear running up his spine as he anticipated what the professor was going to say next.

"Anyway… it's all there. What we did. What we found. You can read it for yourself, and you will understand. The main thing is that you forgive me and Nakamura and the others for what we did, and also forgive particularly me, Jun-san, for laying this burden on you like this."

Jun shook his head.

"*Sensei*, you don't need to..." he began, but the older man gestured for him to be silent.

"Nevertheless. But Jun-san, please listen carefully. If anything happens to me, you must get out of here at once. You will not be safe. None of the others were... and you won't be either. You must leave the university and get far away. Tell no one where you are going. Keep the drive safe. Above all things... keep it safe. Do you understand what I am saying? What I'm asking of you?"

Jun looked down at the little red flash drive and then at his professor.

"*Hai*. I understand. Please don't worry about it. I'll look after it. But I'm sure you don't...."

The professor held up his hand again.

"I do... worry. That's why I am talking to you about this tonight and entrusting you with this task. If anything happens, it's up to you, Jun-san. It is up to you to ensure this information gets out and gets into the right hands."

Jun and the professor talked for a while longer, but Suzuki was not going to be drawn as to his research or whatever it was that was on the flash drive, which he forbade Jun-san to look at in the strongest terms unless something happened to him and certain other conditions were met.

He left that night with the little flash drive in his pocket and a feeling of foreboding in his heart, which had only grown stronger as the day of the conference approached. And then, like a long-anticipated tsunami, the worst had happened.

That night in far-away Hirado on the southern island of Kyushu, Jun had walked out to the sea and watched a sharp crescent moon rise like a bright curved blade over the quiet waters of the Sea of Japan. It reminded him of an old poem he had heard somewhere long ago written by a masterless samurai at the end of the Meiji period:

> *My blade sings*
> *the soft song*
> *of long past days.*
> *Who will listen now though?*
> *On a boat in the moonlight,*
> *I lower it into the waters.*

Chapter 11

Shadows

Chief Inspector Yamashita and Detective Sergeant Yokota parked their car unobtrusively a few hundred meters away from the entrance to *Odawara Iaido Dojo,* and sat waiting for a while until the afternoon classes were scheduled to start and they could be sure that at least one of the men they wanted to talk to would be present. As they waited, they watched as students arrived one by one, most dressed in their school uniforms and carrying large bags with their carefully folded *iaido* uniforms and other equipment.

A few of them carried their practice swords in black canvas bags, but most left them at the *dojo* rather than have to carry them around all day, where they tended to attract the unwelcome attention of the police.

Over the centuries, several rulers had tried to disarm the population with various levels of success, however, it was not until 1876 that the samurai were formally banned from wearing the *daisho*, or the matched pair of swords that were the major signifier of their class, and at the same time the standing army and the police force was formed to guarantee security to the citizenry. Yet the only time the entire Japanese population had been successfully disarmed was in

1946, when the occupying Americans led by General MacArthur had ordered the confiscation of all swords, resulting in over three million of them being voluntarily handed over.

Students of *iaido* were allowed to carry their weapons only to and from a class, but they had to be either wrapped or in a bag or both.

"This takes me back, I can tell you," said Yokota, a burly man in his late thirties with a buzz cut and the thickly muscled arms that *kendo* practitioners of his rank tended to have, that being one of the main reasons that Yamashita had asked him to come along on this particular interview. *Kendo*, the 'way of the sword,' was one of the most popular sports for police officers in Japan, and there were a number of police *dojo* where they practiced and where some of the leading experts in the country tended to belong. Yokota, now a fifth *dan* practitioner and someone who had studied *kendo* since elementary school, was high up and very respected in this community, and was also very familiar, as many senior *kendoka* were, with the art of *iaido*. If anyone could spot even the slightest thing unusual in the place they were about to enter, it was Yokota, who also had the advantage of having the kind of face that struck mortal fear into a wide range of the criminal fraternity.

"I imagine it does," said Yamashita, looking at his watch.

"Yes… I trained here a few times. When I was in high school," he said a little wistfully, buttoning his coat against the cold wind outside.

"What did you think of it?"

Yokota smiled. "Think of it? You mean apart from the fact two crims ran it?"

"Apart from that."

"Well… I dunno. I didn't know they were crims at the time, I mean, I was just a kid. And *iaido* is a bit different. The whole atmosphere of the thing is way different from *kendo*. I mean, in *kendo* you make friends. People do it for fun or just for exercise, and no one rails on you for that at all. You fight in the *dojo,* and the class is often pretty tough, but afterwards you all go for a drink. It's a recreation as well as a serious martial art form. Especially the police clubs…. But this place… hmmm… it was very different. I mean, super strict. I had a friend who used to train here when we were in high school. He did *kendo* like me, but his grandfather was into *iaido* and insisted that the kid practice it. Anyway, he took me along here for a while with him, but I wouldn't say I liked it, to be honest. There was a lot of abuse, and in the end, he quit too. He told me the senior students used to lay into him for the slightest thing, you know, one minute late for class, he would have to mop the floors and do all the tidying up, that sort of thing. And sometimes they smacked him around. Badly too, he told me. So, all up… not a nice place. I didn't like the vibe when I was a kid, either. But I think it was just *this* place mainly. Most *dojo* are fine, and some are really excellent training centers."

Yamashita gave him a sympathetic look. "I know what you mean. It sounds right what you said, given the form on these guys. And it sounds like they've managed to radicalize quite a few others as well, including their kids. Let's just take it easy and see what they have to say."

They made their way up the street and turned into the grounds of the *dojo*, where there was a large single-story farmhouse, one of the last traditional homes in the area, which had been converted into a big one-room practice hall. The walls were all lined with traditional white *shoji* paper windows, and a heavy blue tile roof curved upwards, rendering the structure more imposing than it actually was. These heavy roofs were a double-edged sword themselves, as they were perfect for big typhoons and heavy rains, but in a big enough earthquake, they could cause the whole house to collapse under their weight in a second.

When they opened the main door and stepped inside, the first thing that hit them, despite the cold outside, was the stench of human sweat.

"Smells like home," Yokota murmured to his boss, and Yamashita nodded. In his youth, he and his brother had practiced *judo*, and the smell of a *dojo* was something he was quite familiar with, like many Japanese men. But Yamashita had preferred music and *shogi*, the Japanese game of chess, and hadn't pursued it very seriously past elementary school.

Inside on the polished wooden floor, the *iaido* class was in full swing, and five senior students were performing a simultaneous *kata* exercise watched by one of the instructors, whom Yamashita recognized from his police report as one Kentaro Odawara, the younger of the two Odawara brothers. As they stood watching the students perform, they noticed the man shoot a quick look at them, sum up who they were at a glance, and then turn his attention back to the students and ignore them.

"He looks a little nervous, don't you think?" Yamashita murmured to his colleague, who nodded in response.

When the *kata* was finished, the two police officers walked over to Odawara and showed him their warrant cards, which seemed to make absolutely no impression on him at all, so if he was concerned by the sudden arrival of the police at his premises, he gave no indication of it, something that Yamashita knew was a common tell in the more hardened class of criminals.

Without a word, Odawara, a tall, wide-shouldered brute of a man with a bald pate and a five o'clock shadow, gestured to one of the students who had just finished the *kata* to take over, and led the two officers back over to the doorway as if he was about to show them out the way they had come.

"Whatever you want, make it quick," he barked at them when they were alone.

Yamashita gave him his sweetest smile, which he was sure annoyed the man even more. The art of good interrogation, and for Yamashita it *was* an art, lay in staying calm and asking good questions. Setting traps for the unsuspecting, a lot like *shogi*, which he also played at a very high level. As his old boss used to tell him - "Never raise your voice to a suspect." And so far, he never had.

"So nice of you to spare the time, *sensei*. Let me get to the point then, if you don't mind. We wanted to talk to you about your late nephew, Hisafumi…. We are very sorry for your loss."

Odawara eyed them stone-faced.

"Is that all?" he said in a flat tone.

Yamashita felt his detective sergeant bristling and about to say something, and gestured for him to be silent.

"Actually... no," he said calmly. "We wondered if you might be able to help us with our inquiries as to his... associates. It seems your nephew was, well ... how shall I put it, *involved* in a right-wing political group. Did you know that? In fact, several of your students here are also members of the same little group, I believe. Isn't that interesting? And due also to the fact that he murdered an esteemed academic with a sword...." Yamashita glanced over at the rows of students with their shining practice swords going through a *kata* where they cut down three imaginary opponents at once. "We just thought you might be able to shed some light on this?"

Yamashita smiled again and waited. He was more than used to dealing with people like Odawara, and the man's obvious physical strength and surly attitude didn't bother him in the slightest. In the end, he would always win, and he knew that.

Odawara stared at him and shrugged, but otherwise made no answer.

Yamashita said nothing either and continued to look the man in the eye, and finally, Odawara blinked.

"I don't know anything about any political groups. We're an *iaido dojo*. That's all," he said gruffly.

Yamashita looked at his detective sergeant, who was glaring at Odawara with unmasked contempt, and raised a questioning eyebrow.

"Ah... I see. Now that is strange. I mean, after all... you used to be in one yourself, isn't that correct? The *tatenokai*?

The 'Shield Society'... I believe that's what you used to call yourselves?"

Odawara looked at the floor.

"A long time ago. And nothing to do with what we do here," he muttered.

Yamashita smiled his friendly smile again.

"I see. I'm sure that's true. But you can understand why we, well... how shall I put it... *see a connection*?"

Odawara shrugged again.

"What these kids do in their spare time has nothing to do with me. I told you, we just teach *iaido* here."

"Ah... just *iaido*... So, I wonder then, where do you think your nephew and, er... I'm told your son Keiichi and his friends, get their ideas? They seem remarkably similar to the ones you used to espouse. You know, way back then. And your brother Yasuhiro, too. Perhaps they get them from watching too many old samurai movies?"

At the mention of his son, Odawara bristled even more.

"Leave my son out of it. He's just a university student. If his cousin... took action... that's nothing to do with him."

Yamashita turned to Yokota.

"That's a very interesting turn of phrase, don't you think, detective sergeant? 'Took action.' Now... I would say that's a very *political* turn of phrase..."

"Absolutely, sir," said Yokota. "The kind of phrase one sees all the time in right-wing chat rooms run by filth like this, sir." As he spoke, Yokota moved slightly toward Odawara, and Yamashita noticed the man flinch and move ever so slightly backward in response.

Odawara said nothing though, and Yamashita continued his *soto-voce* interrogation.

"Odawara-san... perhaps you could set our minds at rest on a simple point."

"Like I said. Make it quick. I'm in the middle of a class," he said, jerking his thumb at the students, who were now sitting in a line in the formal *seiza* kneeling position with their sheathed swords at their side watching their instructor go through a new exercise.

"Oh... we don't want to take up your valuable time... I do apologize, *sensei*..." he gave the last word a slightly ironic-sounding tone. "So, tell me... who funds this business?"

This time Odawara started, and looked at him with genuine concern.

"No one. I mean, we do. Student fees..." he stammered.

Yamashita and Yokota exchanged a glance.

"I see. And how much are the monthly fees here?" asked Yamashita, taking a small notebook and pen from his jacket pocket.

"Fees? Depends...."

Yokota glared at him. "If you would like to discuss this at the station, we can do that..."

Odawara swallowed.

"I dunno. About 15,000 yen a month."

"Oh...," said Yamashita. "Very reasonable. So, this little group here today is paying you, let's see, about 10,000 yen or less. Would that be right? For today's class?"

"Something like that," Odawara conceded.

"And how many students do you have?"

"Perhaps something like eighty....."

"I see. Well… I guess it's a living. But after expenses… You have a loan on this place, I believe? And also your house… and children. They can be expensive…."

"What's your point?"

"Well… my point is…" he turned and pointed to the car park just outside where a large late model black Mercedes Benz was parked. "I believe that's your car?"

Odawara made a face.

"Yes. What of it?"

Yamashita smiled. "Well, it's very nice. I wish I could afford a car like that. Don't you, Detective Sergeant Yokota?"

"Yes, sir. I do," agreed the younger man, without shifting his eyes from Odawara's. "It would be interesting to know how this man can afford a car like that."

Before Odawara could answer, Yamashita answered for him.

"Ah, well… there you have it, don't you. I think *sensei* here has some wealthy friends. Would that be right, Odawara-san?"

Odawara shifted nervously. "Perhaps," he muttered. "But that's nothing to do with you. This business is completely above board."

Yamashita nodded and smiled. "So… if we had a look at your books, we would see all donations made by your wealthy friends correctly documented and declared for the purposes of taxation. Right?"

Odawara looked at the floor and said nothing.

"So…" the chief inspector continued in his amiable way. "Let me ask you my original question again. Who funds this business?"

There was a long silence, and the police officers waited without moving.

"You know," said Yamashita. "I believe our friend here may need a bit of a memory enhancer. What do you think, Detective Sergeant Yokota?"

Yokota nodded. "I believe he does, sir."

Yamashita reached into his briefcase and extracted a manilla file which he opened in front of the bemused martial arts instructor and pointed to the figure of the elderly man in the award ceremony photograph that he had previously shown Penelope.

"I believe this man is one of your generous donors, Odawara-san. Wouldn't you agree?"

Odawara's face went several shades paler.

"Courtesy of your website, which your son so helpfully publishes," said Yamashita. "Care to tell us about him? No? Shall I tell you, then? He's pretty well known, you know… in *political* circles… There's that word again, Yokota…."

"Yes, sir."

Yamashita paused again and waited while his words sunk in, but Odawara only shuffled his feet and swore under his breath.

"Now… don't tell me you've forgotten your old friend, Katayama-san? Former vice minister of … what was it? Oh yes… sport, I think. It was quite a while ago, these ministers come and go, don't they? However, did you know he was a very prominent member of the *Shinenkai*? The *New Flame Society*? Were you aware of that, Yokota? A very well-known group of ultra-right-wing politicians, I think?"

"Yes, sir. I believe I am familiar with them."

"And maybe my ears deceived me, but didn't I hear our friend Odawara-*sensei* here tell us he was not involved in politics?"

Odawara growled at him. "He's a family friend. That's all. He's interested in promoting Japanese sports."

Yamashita smiled and turned to Yokota.

"He's interested in promoting Japanese sports, Yokota," the chief inspector repeated.

"That's very interesting, isn't it, sir," said Yokota.

There was silence for a moment, and Odawara shrugged again.

Yamashita took a small step toward the man and closed his folder. "Odawara-san. Let me tell you something, just between us. Let me tell you what I'm interested in…."

"What?" Odawara grimaced and tried to look away, but Yamashita held his gaze.

"I'm interested in finding out why your nephew killed a prominent academic, an innocent man, with a sword. And I am interested in putting *anyone* that helped him, or was in any way connected to his little assassination, in jail for the rest of their lives…" he said quietly.

"And to that end, we will be back to talk to you again… and your brother….."

The two detectives walked back to their car, and Yokota started the engine.

"What do you think?" asked the chief inspector.

Yokota smiled. "I think he just pissed himself, sir."

===================

The day after after the two policemen had finished their meeting with Odawara, Sal arrived home and dumped several bags of shopping from the local supermarket onto his kitchen table, observed by his large orange cat, Watson, who wandered in to check out whether his human had remembered the cat snacks, as he usually did when he went shopping.

Sal may have been a confirmed bachelor, but he liked to cook even if it was just for himself and generally eschewed the prepared food offerings at convenience stores and the like that a lot of other single folk tended to make use of, unless he was particularly busy.

Tonight, he planned to make a simple chicken dish in a cream sauce, a meal he had made many times and which would usually last him a few days. However, it was when he was in the supermarket earlier getting his supplies that his reporter's intuition began to twitch.

He nearly always shopped at the same store near his house, and as he knew where everything was, he could usually get what he needed and be out of there in less than ten minutes. This evening though, as he browsed the cans of peaches he was thinking of using, he noticed something out of the corner of his eye that made him suddenly stiffen. He looked around as casually as he could, as if he was searching for something on the shelf behind him… and there he was.

At the end of the aisle, a man in a dark suit was watching him, and when their eyes ever so briefly made contact, the man had disappeared around the corner out of sight. Sal quietly noted his presence, and went back to looking at some cans on the shelf in front of him and waited to see if the man would make another appearance, which he didn't.

After a few moments, he walked slowly down the aisle, turned the corner, and then doubled back in the direction he had just come from. Sure enough, at the end of the aisle, he found his tail, pretending to look at some fish while watching his prey reflected in the glass wall in front of him.

Sal didn't look at him, picked up a packet of frozen peas from the shelf behind the man, and headed toward the checkout.

"Interesting," thought Sal. He had been followed many times in his career and by people who were much better at it than the man in the dark suit, who had been very easy to spot.

He got the last few items he needed, paid for his shopping, and headed to the car park, where his old black Toyota Harrier was waiting for him.

As expected, he soon spotted the man in the suit enter the car park as well, where he quickly jumped into the passenger side of a black SUV with dark tinted windows.

Sal pretended to check his phone, waited a minute to see if the car would leave before him, and when it didn't, started the engine and headed down the road which led to his house.

He drove along in the expected direction for a few minutes, as if heading home, and then turned left into a little side street to see what they would do. A second later, he saw the black SUV turn the corner after him in his rear-view mirror, and smiled to himself.

"OK, let's have a little fun," he said to himself out loud, and turned another corner.

Born and raised in these little streets, Sal knew the area like the proverbial back of his hand. He began to execute a series of rapid turns in what must have felt like a completely random manner to his pursuer's, sped up until they dropped out of sight, and then shot into the little car park of a nearby temple which he knew could not be seen from the road, and killed his engine so his taillights could not be seen. A second later, he had the pleasure of seeing the SUV shoot past, and allowed himself a smile.

"Sorry lads…. I think I know this place better than you…."

He started his car again, backed out of the car park, and then headed for home in the opposite direction to that of the SUV, arriving just a few minutes later. He didn't have a garage at his house, so he parked in a space he rented just around the corner and carried his shopping back to the house as he usually did.

As it was no secret where he lived, he was not at all surprised when about twenty minutes later, having completed the wild goose chase he had sent them on, he saw from his living room window the black SUV cruise past his house and stop at the end of the street.

"Well, well… I wonder what you boys want…."

He went into his study, returned to the window with his camera and his long-range lens, and snapped a series of photos of the car and its license plate, which he immediately emailed to Chief Inspector Yamashita. He then went back into his kitchen and continued preparing his evening meal.

"Now let's see who you are…" he thought as he stirred in the herbs and popped his old red Le Creuset slow cooker into the oven.

Chapter Twelve.

Tea and *Zazen*

A few days later, Penelope found herself, as she always did early on a Thursday morning, at her regular meditation class at the ancient Engakuji temple, located in the northeast of the city and surrounded by a beautiful forest of pines and cedars. The eight-hundred-year-old temple was especially lovely in the autumn, and many amateur and professional photographers were to be found wandering the grounds at this time of year taking photographs of the elegant old buildings against the dazzling red and gold foliage.

After the class was over, she took the chance to seek out Chief Inspector Yamashita's younger brother Dokan, who was the head monk and probably the abbot of the monastery one day.

As usual, she found the monk sitting on a cushion at the highly polished low table in his spotless office working on the temple's preparations for the New Year, which was always one of the biggest events for temples and shrines throughout Japan.

"Ah, Penny-*sensei*, I was expecting you. Thursday always rolls around so quickly every week though…." he said, rising and turning on his small electric kettle to make them both some tea.

They spent a while talking about her class, which was conducted in English by one of the newer monks, who was from London like Penelope. As the class was in English and Engakuji was quite a famous Zen temple, the class was often attended by many lay and clerical foreigners visiting Japan. Oddly enough, Penelope sometimes found it the only time in the week when she spoke her own language.

As she sipped her green tea, she explained the case she was working on with his brother, in which Dokan was very interested, as well as the background story about the Scroll. The monk, an intelligent and profound thinker in his own right as well as being one of Penelope's best friends, had often been a shedder of light on some of the mysteries in which Penelope had found herself involved over the years, and so she valued this chance to speak with him.

"And all these people are dead?" he said, looking at the photograph of the group of archaeologists that she had produced from the manilla file in her rucksack.

She nodded. "Either dead or disappeared, which is probably the same thing in this case. Professor Suzuki here being the most recent of them."

She pointed at the figure of Suzuki, a tall man in a tweed coat leaning against a tree in the corner of the photograph.

"How appalling…." said Dokan softly, running his hand over his bald pate as he so often did when he saw something that disturbed him. He handed the photograph back to her, and Penelope noted he was dressed in his usual dark blue workman's *jinbei,* the matching tunic and pants that all monks wore when they were not required to be in their typical dark robes.

"And you don't know where this burial site is, nor what they were looking for?" he asked quietly.

Penelope shook her head. "Not a clue so far. It seemed they had good reason to keep the whole thing under wraps, given the government's position on not trespassing into the royal tombs. The only thing we are wondering about is that they could have been looking for Teika no Fujiwara's Jade Scroll, but we really have no idea. The professor's research has been wiped and everyone connected with it... well, you can see for yourself," she said, gesturing at the photograph.

"You realize that if all these men are now dead, you are dealing with some serial killer... or some organization that is adamant about maintaining the secret nature of the tombs? That means you could be placing yourself and your friends in some danger..." he said, looking at her with a concerned expression.

"That has crossed my mind, I must admit. You really think it may be connected to the government?"

Dokan put down his tea and folded his arms.

"Well, that would appear to be the logical deduction to make. But I'm not saying it's the Japanese government or the Imperial Household Agency, you know, the ones who *officially* control access to the tombs. It may simply be some person or group which shares their concern. You know this country, Penny-*sensei*. It's full of weird religious and political groups that have used violence in the past. That's why I'm saying you should be careful."

They were silent for a while, and Penelope watched a red autumn leaf falling from a small maple tree just outside his window.

Dokan picked up his old fountain pen and screwed the lid back on. "Teika no Fujiwara... that's a name I haven't heard since I was at university studying Japanese literature under professors who were much less amiable than you, *sensei*," he smiled. "And that was a long time ago, as you know. Wasn't he responsible for the *hyakunin isshu*?"

Penelope smiled. "You must have been a good student to remember that."

"Actually, I was anything but," laughed Dokan. "I seem to remember that I spent most of my time playing chess and hanging out with girls at the university bar. But we do have a *hyakunin isshu* competition here at Engakuji each New Year as part of the celebrations. Sometimes it's even on the TV...."

Penelope was aware of the temple's connection to the *hyakunin isshu*, or *One Hundred Poems from One Hundred Poets,* which was an ancient anthology of short *waka* poems put together by Teika no Fujiwara in the thirteenth century, and that had been turned into a poetry contest called the *hyakunin issue karuta*, which was held in many places throughout the country, especially at schools and even in people's homes at New Year. During the competition, the contestants would sit on the floor with cards laid out randomly in front of them containing only the second half of the poems (called the *shimonoku*), while the first half (the *kaminoku*) was 'sung' by another person. The first person to find and touch the card with the matching half of the poem won the hand, and the person with the most cards successfully matched at the end of the competition won the contest. Sometimes the poem being read was not among the cards laid out, and the players had to concentrate extremely hard to get the right card. This high-speed search and the difficulty of remembering so many poems made this game especially popular for participants and spectators alike, and had for many centuries.

"Yes," said Penelope, "I remember I came and watched it here myself one year. It's strange because even though I was a literature professor, I don't know half of those poems. Plus, the kids who do it are just so fast…."

"Yeah, I know. They make computers look slow. The human mind is an amazing thing. We Zen people are aware of that, though…" he said, smiling at his guest and pouring her some more of the rich green tea he always served.

"So, this fragment of a letter… the Teika Fragment, you called it? It's the only record we have of the Jade Scroll?"

Penelope nodded. "Yep. Without that, we wouldn't have even known it existed. If indeed, it did. I don't know… maybe he just made it up."

Dokan gave her a sideways look. "I would say that's unlikely. If his proposal to write an imperial history using the information from the scroll was perceived as a threat to the emperor, then most likely the other party was aware of the existence of the Scroll. Otherwise, it's not a threat, is it? No… I would say it existed, and that old Teika probably had it. What it said about the early Japanese monarchs is another matter, however. That… we really don't know."

Penny had to admit the wily Zen cleric had put his finger on a critical point, the exact same one that Professor Xu had formulated. The Scroll must have existed at some point, there was truth to that.

"Tell me," continued Dokan, picking up the photograph of the murdered archaeologists. "Why do you think it's buried in a tomb, wherever it is? And why do you think it is an imperial tomb?"

Penelope shrugged. "I'm not really. Professor Suzuki and his group were all researchers into the ancient Imperial family, so I'm assuming it is an imperial tomb. If it is, it would be the perfect hiding place, wouldn't it? A place that no one would dare to enter. It makes sense."

The monk tapped on a book on his desk with his pen and looked lost in thought.

"You know…" he said finally. "If I were going to hide something valuable, there is an alternative to going to the trouble of burying it. I could, for example, give it to someone I trusted. Or maybe entrust the whereabouts of the hiding place to that person. I don't know if I would just bury it somewhere and not tell anyone where it was. Especially if it was something as important as the Scroll, which was a priceless heirloom even back then."

Penelope looked at him carefully. "So… what you are saying is…."

The monk smiled and looked up. "I'm saying… that someone knew, or even knows… where it is."

====================

One morning a few days after her conversation with Dokan, Penelope had another visitor, this time someone she had been expecting. Professor Xu, late, flustered and dressed in her usual white blouse and black suit, knocked on her front door.

Any visitor coming to her house for the first time, and today that was her, immediately faced a few challenges, the major one being the ability to find it.

Penelope's old house was in a quiet and very traditional little neighborhood of Kamakura not far from the central library, located in a warren of tiny little streets lined with similar old wooden houses, most of which dated back to the post-war Showa period and some before even that. Apart from little houses, whose proximity to each other meant that privacy was something of a pipe dream and where everyone not only knew everyone else but spent an inordinate amount of time gossiping about them, there were a dozen or so tiny shops selling mainly foodstuffs, and this was where you were meant to do your shopping, as going further afield to some large supermarket in town was seen as an act of unforgivable treachery. The look on the face of this evening's dinner guest as she arrived almost half an hour late confirmed the fact that nothing, including the times, had changed at all.

"This place is not so easy to find, is it?" said Professor Xu with a pleasant smile as she gratefully accepted the glass of wine that Penelope proffered. "Usually, I can find any address using Google Maps…" she said, waving her phone in the air, "but this place… I had to ask two of your neighbors where you lived. Luckily, they knew you…."

Penelope laughed. "Yeah, they all know me. And I know them, bless them. Plus, I'm the only foreigner half of them have ever met, let alone had a conversation with. So, my fame does have its uses sometimes. Don't worry though, everyone who comes here says the same thing. Maybe I should put up a sign or something. It was the same for me the first time I tried to find this place. And half the time when I invite someone, I give up and go and meet them at the station."

Professor Xu laughed. "Oh well, at least I'm not the only one then. I can never get used to the fact that half the places in Japan, especially little places like this, have no street names and that sometimes like twenty different houses have the same numbers. Even in Shanghai, and that's not a place famous for getting around easily, this kind of thing would be regarded as a kind of cruel joke."

Penelope nodded. "Yes, I know exactly what you mean. This area is built to laugh at things like Google Maps. Anyway, make yourself at home, I've lots to tell you."

Over dinner the two women discussed the case in detail, and Penelope brought Professor Xu up to date on the latest developments. After a dessert of fresh fruit, cheese, and a glass of vintage tawny port, which the Professor claimed to have never had before, she came to the point of her visit.

"Anyway, like I told you on the phone, I talked to my mother about the photograph. Since the same one has been hanging on the wall of my father's study for the last twenty years, she had no trouble remembering it, and she remembered the men in it too."

"Your mother was with him in Japan?"

Xu shook her head. "According to her, my Dad worked with these same archaeologists on several digs, not just in Japan but also in China. Sometimes they came to our house. It was a kind of academic exchange. However, she could not remember where he took this particular photograph."

The professor sipped her port. "This is really very good, you know. I think I am going to have to get a bottle next time I go to a department store or something. Yes, anyway... according to my mother, this photograph was taken at a burial mound, but we don't know where. It *could* have been on one of his first trips to Japan though, but she wasn't sure. She said she would have a dig around in his old diaries and see if she could find out."

"Well, that's a step forward at least. At least we know they were at a burial mound. Did he tell her what the purpose of the dig was?"

"Well... yes and no. Apparently, he was only called in at the end, like on the final day. He never saw the inside of what they were excavating, he said. According to her, he told her only Professor Suzuki and Professor Nakamura went inside, but he said they were very excited by the whole thing, and that he was shown a piece of jade with some inscriptions on it, which from what he said to my mother sounded a lot like yours."

"Did he say if they found anything else?"

Professor Xu shook her head.

"She didn't know. But he did tell her to keep quiet about it, because he said they didn't have the proper permissions. I have to say, it does sound like Japan, but we can't be sure. China has a lot of red tape too. Anyway, she wasn't supposed to breathe a word about it. He was actually very good friends with both professors, especially Nakamura, who often stayed with us in Shanghai."

Penelope sighed, and they were silent for a while.

"Do you think this is really all about the Scroll?" asked Professor Xu.

Penelope looked at the ceiling and crossed her arms. "Maybe. I can't think of what else it could be about. That's what Enrico in Osaka thinks too, as you know. It's kind of the Holy Grail for academics in this field, right? According to him, and maybe you too, it would be the only thing that could drive these men to such lengths…."

"An illegal excavation?"

"Yes, if that's what it was."

Xu nodded. "Yeah… that's true. I have to confess that if I knew where it was… I would probably move heaven and earth to get to it as well. It's just… well, it just answers all the questions. A detailed history of the very beginnings of Japan. Who they were. Where these first rulers came from, and God knows what else. It's like the Rosetta stone in lots of ways. China is different in that way. We don't know everything, but it was always a country with court-appointed historians and an old and established bureaucracy that produced a massive amount of public records. Although we still have lots of questions, we also have a lot more than Japan does about its so-called 'legendary' past. If we had the Scroll… we might be able to finally know."

Penelope poured her another glass of port, despite her guest's protestations.

"We might indeed. You know… a friend of mine, he's a monk actually at Engakuji, he told me something interesting the other day."

"What was that?"

"Well... he reckons the Scroll wasn't buried at all," said Penelope, recalling her conversation with Dokan.

"Really? Is he a historian?" asked Xu, intrigued.

Penelope laughed. "No. He's even better than that. Or should I say more useful? He's just a very shrewd judge of human nature."

Xu threw up her hands. "Oh, don't apologize for that. Actually, it accounts for half the major historical finds worldwide. If you can figure out how people think, it's often incredibly useful. So, what does he think happened to it?"

Penelope gave her an oblique look. "He thinks Teika gave it to someone he trusted."

Xu stared at her. "That's pretty logical when you think about it. I mean, why would you bury it?"

Penelope nodded. "Well, it may well be very logical, but it doesn't really help, does it? How the hell do we know who Teika trusted? It's not like we would know anyone now that's going to jump up and say, "My ancestor was Fujiwara no Teika's best mate, and he gave him a present one day." If anything, if it *was* in a burial mound in Nara, we might have an easier shot at finding it one day...."

Penelope finished her port and stared at the empty glass, a Christmas gift from her late sister in England.

Xu cupped her face in her hand and leaned on the table, lost in thought.

Penelope continued to stare at the glass, remembering her sister's laughing face when they were girls and how they used to run around on Hampstead Heath playing hide and seek with their brother.

She put the glass on the table and looked at Xu.

"Didn't Teika have a family?" she asked quietly.

Xu looked up at her and gave her an intense look, like an idea had suddenly opened very quietly like a flower in her mind.

"Yes… he did. He had many sons and daughters. And their descendants… I've even met some of them…."

Chapter 13.

Family Matters

The man sitting across the table from him was a stranger, but Hasegawa had been informed that morning precisely who he was, and he had also been told, in no uncertain terms, that he was expected to be 'helpful.'

However, looking at the older man sitting in front of him now, though, he got an unpleasant yet very definite feeling that being 'helpful' would be the least of the things required of him.

Hasegawa's father, a senior politician in the ruling party who had once held several important ministerial portfolios, had made a phone call to him that morning, an event of such shocking rarity that Hasegawa had been unable to finish his breakfast. His father was an austere and very traditional man, intensely proud of his family's achievements and status over the generations, where successive members of his family had served the government going back to the days of the *shogun,* the ancient military rulers of Japan.

He was also a man who valued loyalty above all else, and brooked no association with anyone who violated that particular code, least of all his younger son, whose appointment to the position of associate professor in the department of archaeology at Hassei university, the same department formerly run by the recently deceased Professor Suzuki who had been his immediate boss, had been made very largely because of his family's connections and also aided by a large and anonymous donation to the university that had been made once that position had been confirmed.

Hasegawa *père* had, in his turn, been the recipient of another phone call the day before from someone whom he not only respected but feared, and had hastened to contact his son with explicit instructions to arrange an appointment with Katayama-*sensei*. This man, he informed his pudgy younger son, whom he actually rather disliked and absolutely mistrusted, was an old and esteemed colleague. He was to meet him at his office in Nagatacho, the center of the Japanese political world in Tokyo, where he was to be both on time and *as cooperative as possible,* if the family's good name and the fortunes of his elder brother, an aspiring younger politician who had taken over his father's legislative seat in the House of Representatives, was going to see a future. Did he understand? His son had sworn he did, and his father had hung up without a word of goodbye.

At the appointed hour of 10 a.m. on the dot, he had presented himself at Katayama's offices. The office was on the tenth floor of a modern office building housing the headquarters of a well-known life insurance company and was surrounded by various important government buildings and just a stone's throw from the Sakuradamon gate of the Imperial Palace.

After waiting for a few minutes on a large black leather sofa in the elegant outer office, where a pretty young secretary had bade him wait while she attended to her laptop, the inner door had opened, and one of the most enormous men that he had ever seen, a hulking possibly ex-sumo wrestler that was almost bursting out of his dark suit, had approached him and made a deep bow with his hands at his sides in the most formal of ways. Whoever he was, his role in life was pretty clear - he was one of Katayama's security team, and probably one of his gofers. As he escorted him into his boss's opulent office, Hasegawa had no fears whatsoever that his boss was safe. Whether he was going to be, was another question.

The office was large, as he had expected, and looked out in one direction over the gardens of the Palace and the road that ran up towards one of the eight gates that surrounded it and in the other towards the elegant old Hibiya Park and the Toranomon business district. It was well appointed, with a couple of matching leather sofas on either side of a glass coffee table, both of which sat in front of a vast desk. In the corner of the room was a large Japanese flag, such as one often found in politician's offices, and around the walls a series of pictures of former Japanese prime ministers and other dignitaries stared down, including a photograph of their Royal Highnesses the Emperor Reiwa and his wife the Empress Masako in formal attire, and another of Bando Masakichi, whom Hasegawa knew had been in charge of his father's political faction within the ruling party, and whom he knew people quietly referred to as the *kuromaku,* or 'Puppet Master.'

A sudden understanding of exactly who this man was slowly dawned on the rattled Hasegawa, and he felt his blood run cold.

Katayama-*sensei*, a rail-thin silver-haired man with small, somewhat reptilian eyes and dead-white hands with long elegant fingers that reminded Hasegawa of a skeleton, waved him to one of the sofas, and a second later the pretty young secretary appeared bearing glasses of hot *hogicha,* a dark tea well known for its various health benefits and which the younger man was secretly grateful for.

The older man made his way slowly from behind the desk and gave Hasegawa a polite bow.

"Thank you so much for sparing the time this morning… it's Associate Professor Hasegawa… is that correct?" said Katayama, lowering himself carefully into the plush Italian leather of the sofa.

"Yes, that's correct, *sensei*," said Hasegawa with a slight bow, using the polite term *sensei,* which was extended to politicians and lawyers, as well as teachers. "My father informed me that I might be of some service?"

"Ah, yes, your father. An esteemed colleague of many years. I've missed him since he retired. But it is still nice to know that he is available when the need arises," Katayama smiled weakly. "You don't know how much pleasure it gives us older folk when we can work with the children and grandchildren of our old friends. It gives one a feeling of… continuance, in this unstable age. My own son is now in politics as well… as is your elder brother Yusuke? Is that right?"

"Yes, *sensei*. I'm extremely grateful for the help you have so kindly extended to my family for such a long time…." he said as politely as he could.

The older man gave him a sideways look as if nothing could be more natural and waved away his thanks.

"Not at all. In fact, you are in a position where you might be of some use to us... Could I ask you a few questions about your university? Hassei, I believe? A nice old place. I think we have sent several donations to it over the years...."

Hasegawa knew for a fact that one of those donations had been for his benefit, and he was equally aware that Katayama knew it too. The younger man sighed inwardly. Such is my lot in life, he thought. Dependent on my family and these old men. Now the bill is about to come....

"So, I hear you are in the Department of Archaeology at Hassei? Is that right?" said the older man with a dignified smile.

"Yes, *sensei*. That's right."

"Such a shame about Professor Suzuki. You knew him well?"

Hasegawa nodded.

"You know... I want to talk to you about a private matter...and I know I can trust you not to speak of our conversation...."

Katayama gave him another sidelong look, and the younger man nodded that this was indeed so. *Silent as the grave sensei, you can depend on me...*

"Very good. I think you will go far, young man. As so many of your family have...." He didn't need to add 'with our help,' as that was clearly understood.

"So, tell me. Did Professor Suzuki, whom you knew so well, have anyone he especially... trusted?" asked Katayama in an innocent-sounding voice, as if he was inquiring about the late professor's health.

"Trusted? I'm sorry, I'm not sure what you mean, *sensei*. He was a very nice man. I think he trusted all his staff and students.

Katayama looked out the window at the blue sky, and when he looked back, Hasegawa could tell he was annoyed.

"Perhaps I'm not making myself clear. It's a problem for us old folk. We speak so vaguely sometimes. Let me put it another way. Did the professor have anybody he might have entrusted with… *important information*. Something he might have preferred no one else knew about. Someone… close to him. Is that clearer?"

The question hung in the air like the Sword of Damocles, and Hasegawa realized, to his dismay, that his career hung there too. He thought as rapidly as possible, running through all the people in his department. And then a face somehow floated up from his memory. And then an old conversation he had been a part of.

Where was it?

A ramen restaurant near the university. With his old classmate Tomo, who was working at Kyoto University as a tutor now… What did he say?

"Yeah, that guy. Old Suzuki always gave him the plum jobs… He even got an associate professorship right after he graduated. God knows why"

And the face…. Suddenly it had a name.

"Jun Miyamoto," he blurted out. "He was the professor's main research assistant."

The older man smiled. "Now… you're sure of this? We wouldn't want to be going off on any wild goose chases, would we."

No, we wouldn't, Hasegawa thought.

"He's an associate professor, like me. But I hear he was very close to old Suzuki. Worked with him since he was an undergraduate. Went on all his digs with him, helped him with his research. He was... important to the professor, at least that's what everyone said."

At least that's what my drunk friend who was jealous of him said.

Katayama looked out the window and then back again at the sweating face of the young professor.

"Very good, that is indeed what I needed to know. I knew you could help. So... where might I find this young man? I would like to speak with him immediately if possible."

Hasegawa swallowed hard. "I have no idea, *sensei*... but I can find out if you like."

Katayama nodded. "Well... I *would* like that. That would be most helpful. Especially if you could get this information... today? Would that be possible?"

Hasegawa nodded emphatically. "I'm sure I could do that, *sensei*. I'll make some inquiries. Do you want his home address?"

Katayama said he did, and with that got slowly to his feet to indicate that their meeting was over.

"Thank you, professor. You've been most helpful. Please pass on my respects to your esteemed father."

He pushed a button on his desk, and a second later the door opened and the sumo wrestler appeared.

"Please show Professor Hasegawa to the elevator, Akira-san. Thank you again, professor. I shall await your phone call."

He passed the panicked young man a business card, and a moment later Hasegawa was in the elevator headed to the ground floor.

He emerged into the tree-lined autumn street, where the last of the bright yellow ginkgo leaves clung to their branches in the cold breeze. He took a deep breath, swore loudly to himself, and headed to the nearest subway station feeling like a man who had just dodged a bullet.

He rode the subway back to Ebisu station and transferred to the express train to Kamakura, the same one he had taken up to Tokyo that morning. On his way, he texted several colleagues who had known Miyamoto, the professor's favored factotum, but the news was not encouraging. Apparently, no one had seen Miyamoto since the day after the professor's death, and he had been gone now for nearly three weeks.

In the end, he had called someone he knew in the university's administrative department, who confirmed that Professor Miyamoto had taken a sudden leave of absence 'for family reasons.' No, they were not aware of the date of his return.

Hasegawa alighted at Kamakura station and made his way to the university, where he went to the office of Professor Kimura, who had been standing in as the Head of Department since the death of his predecessor.

Kimura waved him inside, and he sat on a folding chair in front of the professor's desk, overflowing with papers and books as usual and with hardly room enough for the little notebook computer he favored, and as always, Hasegawa felt that he was no friend. He wondered if Kimura might have known how he had gained his appointment, and that as an old-school and famously meticulous academic he found people like Hasegawa, with their deep family connections and money, unpalatable. But he also wasn't going to let that stop him from dealing with this underling in a professional manner.

"And you say Miyamoto borrowed some important files from you? Is that right?" asked the elderly professor, who continued to work on his emails without looking up.

"Yes, *sensei*. That's right. It's really critical that I speak with him. Otherwise, I cannot finish my presentation for the conference in Singapore next week.

"I see, and you've tried calling him?"

"Yes. No answer. I hear he took family leave or something. So, I was wondering if you could give me his home address? I could pop over and see him that way. Maybe he's just changed his phone number or something…"

Kimura looked up and stared at him like his inquiry was suspicious in some way, but then he nodded, and after searching through his online files, which the university had given him access to as a Department Head, he wrote down an address on a slip of paper.

"This is the address I have. Anything else?" he said coldly.

"No, *sensei*. Thank you. That's most helpful."

Hasegawa knew there was no time to waste if he was going to be able to report to Katayama the same day as he had promised, so he immediately hailed a passing taxi outside the old black wrought-iron gates of the university and gave the driver the address.

Fortunately, it was close by, and about twenty minutes later, he was walking towards a site he knew well in a quiet residential area to the northeast of the city, quite close to the ancient Zen temple of Jomyo-ji.

As a historian, he was well aware of the temple's past and its importance. It had been founded in 1188 by a famous Buddhist priest as one of the first Zen monasteries in Japan and was an important place for the Rinzai school of Zen, one of the three main schools of the sect. It had also been deeply connected to the Ashikaga family, who had later ruled as *shogun* from their base in Kyoto, and that according to one of the more important historical records, the *Taiheiki*, had been the place where Ashikaga Tadayoshi had been imprisoned and later poisoned in the fourteenth century.

None of this grisly history seemed evident today, and the graceful old homes in the streets near the temple felt peaceful and somehow quietly imbued with the tranquillity that often accompanies places near those dedicated to the art of meditation, or *zazen*.

After wandering around for several minutes looking for the house, he found an elegant old wooden home hidden down a little street by the long wall of the temple itself, which had a faded wooden nameplate where the weathered name of *Miyamoto* was just legible.

He pushed the buzzer underneath it, and after a few moments a woman's voice answered, and he was admitted into a small garden in front of the house.

Miyamoto's mother was a frail woman in her early eighties wearing an old brown kimono with a traditional dark purple apron over it.

They talked at the door, and the elderly lady did not ask him to come in.

"Ah..." she said, after listening to his made-up story about the need to retrieve his files. "I'm so sorry to hear that you have been inconvenienced like this. That's very inconsiderate of him... he should have returned them to you before he left..." she gave him a little bow and lowered her eyes to the ground by way of apology.

"Oh... he left?"

"Yes... he said he had to go away for a while. He asked me not to tell anyone, though... I'm so sorry. He's usually not so... mysterious, you know. But then... all this business with Professor Suzuki. Such a lovely man. And so good to Jun.... You know, Jun's father died when he was small. I think he thought of the professor like he was... I don't know...." She looked away over the lovely little garden, and Hasegawa knew in his heart what she meant. He often felt like he hadn't had a father either.

"I see. That's a shame. You see, I have this important conference coming up... and these files... well, without them... I don't know what to do...."

He looked at her beseechingly, and saw in her eyes that she was wavering.

"I don't need to bother him for more than a moment. I just need to see him and get these documents... that's all. He's probably just forgotten he promised to return them after... well, you know, Professor Suzuki...."

The old lady nodded. "Nevertheless, he should have been more careful. It's so rude of him not to have considered other people like this. But... the problem is he's not in Kamakura at the moment. So, there isn't much I can do...."

"He's not in Kamakura?" said Hasegawa, his heart sinking.

Mrs. Miyamoto shook her head.

"No, I'm so sorry. It's strange, but you are the second person in the last few days who needed to contact Jun very urgently. It's really too bad of him to run out of here and not make sure he was inconveniencing people. He's at our old family house in Nagasaki Prefecture.... would you like the phone number?"

Chapter 14

The Rain Child

"You do realize that you are talking about something that happened eight hundred years ago, don't you?" said Professor Xu with a confused look. "I mean... the chances... the chances of being able to find anything today... are like less than zero...."

"I know. But isn't that what makes it interesting?" said Penelope smiling.

Xu shook her head. "Well... interesting... that's one word for it..."

Penelope's idea, which she propounded to Professor Xu in her living room that evening, was as practical as it was completely unlikely. Nevertheless, Xu was intrigued by this unusual approach that the retired literature professor was insisting on, and finally agreed that considering the lack of a better idea, it might just be worth giving it a shot. After all, they had nothing to lose and no other course to follow. She was right, too, that as a professional historian, it was a fascinating thread on which to pull.

Over the next few days that autumn, as the leaves turned gold and red on the old maple tree in Penelope's garden, the professor took some leave from her university and moved into the spare bedroom with a pile of books and her laptop, and they set about enthusiastically pursuing what they both had to admit was a crazy idea, which was that Teika no Fujiwara, the greatest poet of his age, had not buried the Scroll at all, but rather entrusted it to a member of his family. If so, and if his descendants were still alive, could it be possible that the family had kept the scroll hidden all these years, perhaps unaware of what it was?

As neither of them was an expert on the Fujiwara family, Penelope had contacted an old friend through her university, the novelist Sachie Okutani, whom she remembered had written her Ph.D. thesis on Teika under her supervision decades before, and asked her to join them. She was an old friend, and they still occasionally met for lunch a few times a year, and whenever one of her new books was published, Penelope usually went to the book signing, which was often held at the old Maruzen store in Nihonbashi in the center of Tokyo. There she lined up with everyone else to get her copy signed, and to meet the now famous author, who mainly wrote novels on historical themes and whose books had become the basis of several television dramas over the years.

She also roped in Fei, who, even more so than Professor Xu, thought the whole idea was an insane waste of time, and together the four women spent the next two days reconstructing the main lines of Teika's family and also making a lot of educated guesses as to what may have happened over the eight hundred years that had passed since the poet died.

Penelope divided her time between cooking for the group and researching herself, and to the delight of all her cats, who loved company, they all stayed the night, with Xu and

Sachie sharing futons in the spare bedroom, and even Fei, who only lived next door, taking over the sofa in the living room.

The more they researched though, the more Xu and Sachie began to think that there might indeed be something in Penelope's offbeat approach to the problem after all. The only one who consistently questioned what they were doing was Fei, who delighted in the devil's advocate and arch-contrarian role.

"You know Fei," said Xu at one point, in response to one of Fei's less-than-flattering outbursts about the unlikeliness of their project's success. "Do you know how they found Troy?"

Fei shook her head, and the others looked up at her from what they were doing.

"It's an interesting story. Heinrich Schliemann, a German businessman and polyglot, told his parents when he was seven years old that one day he was going to find the city of Troy, which he had read about at school in Homer's Odyssey and Iliad, something all schoolboys read in those days. I guess it's not many kids with that tenacity that their childhood dreams extend right into their old age. But that was what Schliemann was like, I think. He was a pioneer in the field of archaeology in the nineteenth century, when the science was really just finding its feet, and talented and persistent amateurs made many great discoveries. Anyway, Schliemann was a real one-of-a-kind. For example, he used to say he could learn any language in just six weeks, and when he died, it was said he knew at least fourteen fluently."

"Anyway, regarding Troy," she said with a smile and warming to her theme. "For a start, no one believed in it. The stories Schliemann had read in Homer, and the city it talked about and Achilles and Paris and Helen and all that, were all thought to be myths. No one actually believed they existed, and no one thought the old Greek stories that had been passed down by Homer thousands of years ago could possibly be true.... Until Schliemann proved that they were. He found Troy principally guided by clues provided in Homer. And that's a true story... So, what we're doing is maybe not so weird after all."

They were all encouraged by this story, but when a few days later they sat back and surveyed the fruits of their labors, they had to admit they had hit a brick wall.

Their results, portrayed on a large whiteboard in Penelope's living room that was now covered with tiny lines, arrows, names and post-it notes, was a marvel of what Sachie rather archly called a 'complexity breakfast.'

"So, girls," said Sachie, who was a plump middle-aged woman in a purple cardigan who wore her waist-length long hair tied back in a ponytail. "Now you can see the problem. I hit this same kind of wall with Teika when I was writing my thesis. So, let me sum it up for you." She pointed at the whiteboard with the butt end of a kitchen spatula.

"First of all, the old bugger had *twenty-seven* children, mainly with his various concubines." She pointed her kitchen tool at a long list on the side of the board. "These kids then divided after his death into three warring schools of poetry, the Nijo, the Reizei, and the Kyogoku schools. Naturally enough, all the kids wanted to cash in on the fact that Daddy was the greatest poet in the land, which they did.

The Kyogoku school later merged with the Reizei, who were in the ascendency for a couple of centuries, and then they got hit with a lawsuit from the Nijo faction, and forced to hand over all of Daddy's documents. Then they *and* the Nijo school produced hordes of forgeries to attack each other, and in the end the Nijo group also hit the skids when their leader was killed whilst on his travels. So, although the descendants of the Reizei school are still extant, and I've met a few of them, there is *no way* they would not know what they had if they did have the Scroll, and *they,* most likely and as they are very nice people, would have donated it to the nearest museum."

Fei nodded in agreement.

"She's right. There is nothing to indicate that any of these groups had the Scroll, and since there was a war over Teika's property back in the day, the Scroll would definitely have come to light or at least have been mentioned. I think this is a dead end, ladies."

She picked up Marmalade, one of Penelope's four cats, and sat stroking the large tabby while the others stared morosely at the whiteboard.

Professor Xu waved the notebook she had been using in the air and stood up.

"What about this guy?" she said, pointing to the name of one Nijo Tameuji, the eldest of Teika's sons. "Wouldn't it make sense that he would have given it to him? He was the eldest after all, and that counted for a great deal back then."

Sachie nodded. "That would have been my guess too. He was pretty busy mounting a lawsuit against another family member though, and deeply unpopular by all accounts. Also, one of his main descendants was an alcoholic and wasted a lot of the family fortune. Like I said, no hint they ever had the Scroll. Nor that they were even interested in it. Which was a point you could make about all of them, in fact. The Scroll was ancient and extremely valuable. Even the Emperor wanted it, probably either to destroy it or keep it out of anyone else's hands. I reckon we would have known about it if these guys had owned it. There would have been some record of it. But as things stand, there's nothing, and no indication that Teika would have bequeathed it to any of them, particularly one of the members of the three schools, who were all out for the fame and money."

There was silence in the room for a long time until, in the end, Penelope stood up and pointed to the list of names of all Teika's children.

"You're right, I think, especially when you say that if these fame-hounds had got their hands on the Scroll we would have known about it. So, what if they *didn't* know about it? What if Teika managed to make it disappear, leaving them to think the same as us, that it had either been destroyed or never existed?"

They all looked at her.

"That's all just speculation too, Penny," said Sachie.

"True… but… let's speculate for a while," said Penelope amiably, tapping the children's names with the end of her pen. "Now…this may sound like just another silly question, but do we know which one of these he liked best?"

Sachie and Professor Xu laughed.

"No… sorry, we don't," said Professor Xu, rather flatly.

Penelope stared at the board.

"Do we know which of these kids he had with his wife? I mean, his natural, legal kids?"

Sachie underlined several names. "These were the ones we know of. Some of them did not survive until adulthood. And some of these others… could have been adopted into the family too…."

"Adopted?" asked Penelope.

"Pretty common practice in those days," said Sachie.

Penelope shook her head and picked up her mug of tea which had long since gone cold. She knew the novelist was right, and adoption just made the whole issue even more complicated.

"OK," she said. "If we don't know which of the kids he liked, do we know which of their mothers he liked best? I mean… I know he had quite a harem to choose from."

"Again…" said Professor Xu this time. "We don't know. It was also really common for a man of Teika's status, especially as a part of the dominant Fujiwara family, to have loads of concubines. It was a kind of status symbol. The Fujiwara controlled the imperial line for centuries and married their daughters into it for political purposes. Often when the emperors were too young to rule, a Fujiwara regent would do it for them. Even the current Emperor is descended from them. Supposedly," she added.

Penelope turned and looked at Sachie.

"OK. Side issue… maybe. Do you remember when you were a graduate student Sachie-san when we went to see that Noh play? Wasn't it because it was about Teika? You wanted to see it because you were writing about it in your doctoral thesis? Do you remember? It was a love story, wasn't it?"

Sachie gave her old teacher a surprised look. "Well... oh yes. That was years ago now. *Teika*. Yes, where was it? At the Noh Theatre in Tokyo... I remember now."

Penelope remembered it now as well, vividly. It had been a snowy night in February many years before. Noh, like Kabuki, was an ancient form of Japanese stage drama, even older than its more famous cousin, and often recounted very old tragic stories. She remembered that she and Sachie had met that evening for a quick meal at a coffee shop around the corner from the National Noh Theatre near the old Sendagaya station not far from Shinjuku. She remembered telling Sachie at the time that it was such a shame that so many beautiful plays were done in such an ugly building, which she always thought resembled a bomb shelter rather than a place for artistic expression. Once inside, though, it had been different. *Teika* had been absolutely captivating, sad and magnificent, as the ancient stories so often were.

Sachie began typing something on her laptop.

"Wow, now you are taking me back, Penny-*sensei*. But you know, that's a completely fictional story, don't you? And it was written centuries later. Just a sec, I have it here...."

She spent a few moments looking up the document and then turned the laptop around on the table so the other women could read the synopsis she had found.

"Let me summarize it for you girls, I know this story," said Sachie, pointing to the screen which showed an old Heian period drawing of a woman dressed in the flowing layered robes of the time, her long hair trailing darkly over the tatami mats where she was seated.

"Apparently, once upon a time, a monk and his friends were travelling, and one evening after many days of walking, they finally reached the borders of the old Capital of Kyoto. It started to rain, softly at first and then harder, and the monks ran and sought shelter in the ruins of an old, deserted building. The rain continued, and at some point in the night, a woman appeared in their midst. They are very surprised, of course, and the woman calms them and begins to tell them a story."

"They are, she says, in a building called the Rain Pavilion, which was where the famous poet Teika no Fujiwara used to live. She tells them one of his poems about rain, and then she shows them a gravestone, which is dedicated to an Imperial Princess called Shikishi. She then tells them the love story of Teika and the Princess, and how when Teika stopped coming to see her, she took her life because of a broken heart."

"When Teika heard about this, he was overcome with grief, and spent the rest of his days visiting her grave... Anyway, the monks later find out that the woman who has appeared to them is the ghost of this Lady Shikishi, and they hold a memorial service for her and for Teika to console their spirits."

"Wow... very romantic," said Fei.

"It is, isn't it?" said Sachie. "However, like I said, it was written long afterward, and I guess it's just made up. Teika was a romantic figure in poetry and stories for centuries."

"It's a common plot in many stories, from the Heian period a thousand years ago. Like in the *Tale of Genji*," said Xu.

Penelope agreed. "But that was another thing about Teika. He loved romantic stories, particularly about love in the court. Don't forget, he actually *copied out* the entire *Tale of Genji* in his own hand. A book full of metaphors and obscure poetic references to things. Where the names of many of the characters refer to something about them, rather than being their real names…."

As if a light had suddenly gone off in her head, Penelope spun around and pointed to the name of one of Teika's children on the whiteboard.

"This is a girl, right?" she asked.

"Ameka? Yes. She was his daughter by one of the imperial concubines. I think her mother was a cousin of Teika's. Again, pretty common."

"So, her mother was probably of a good family, right?"

Xu nodded. "Oh, absolutely. She was a Fujiwara too, or at least from one of their branches."

"So, she was of the imperial line, or related to it. Like a princess herself… Do we know what happened to her? The daughter, I mean?" asked Penelope.

Sachie and Xu, being the resident historians, looked at each other and both started tapping on their laptops.

"She became a Buddhist nun, in 1242, the year after Teika died," said Sachie. She wasn't part of any of the three major poetry schools after his death," said Sachie.

"Ameka…" said Penelope softly. "Can I see her name in Japanese? The Chinese characters?"

Professor Xu turned her laptop around so Penelope could see.

雨花

"Ameka. That means 'rain flower,' doesn't it?" said Penelope. "Like in the story about the Rain Pavilion, and all the poems about rain that he wrote. In fact, you could say Teika had a thing about rain, artistically…."

Sachie turned her laptop around too, and pointed at the screen.

"When she took the tonsure and went into the nunnery, she also took a Buddhist name."

They all craned their heads to see her screen.

守花

"Shuka," read Fei. "Protector of Flowers… I think that's a reference to the lotus flower, the symbol of the Buddhist Dhamma, or the truth of the Buddha's teaching."

Xu nodded. "Yes, that's right," she said.

Penelope stood up and smiled at them broadly.

"That's not all it means. 'Shuka'… it can also mean: "Guardian of the Truth."

The three other women stared at her.

"Ladies…" said Penelope, tapping her pen on the name on the whiteboard.

"It's her," she said quietly.

Chapter 15

The Island

For those first setting foot in the tiny seaside town of Hirado, from where Jun Miyamoto's ancestors hailed, history has a little surprise waiting. For once, many, many centuries ago, it had, strangely enough, the distinction of being the first 'international' port in Japan, a distinction which the overwhelming mass of the Japanese population today had now utterly forgotten.

In this country, a land that had been long famous for its isolation from the rest of the world, this was a situation that the rest of its citizens would have found more than a bit unusual, to say the least, as even right up till the middle of the twentieth century it would have been true to say that ninety-nine percent or more of people in Japan had never clapped eyes on a foreigner.

That, however, was not the case in little Hirado, nestled on its sunny peninsula in the most western part of the country.

A port of call for ships since the early Nara period in the sixth century, the local Matsuura clan of the island had been given the right to trade with Song Dynasty China and Korea on behalf of the empire for a lengthy period, and thus it became one of the only places in the country that had contact with the outside world. In scenes that would have been unthinkable in other parts of the country, with quiet regularity the ships of foreign countries came and went, bearing goods and sometimes emissaries from vastly more advanced foreign lands, and where people, for the first time ever, could hear languages other than their own brought by the sea breeze.

In ancient times the journeys in these old, fairly flat-bottomed ships that made it to and from Japan, mainly from the Korean peninsula, were extremely perilous, and the chances of someone surviving the trip, let alone making repeated trips, were low. Ships at the time had no compass, no idea of longitude and latitude, and thus no idea where they were. If the weather turned quickly, as it so often did, particularly in the typhoon season, they were quite often blown hopelessly off course or simply rolled over and sank with the loss of all hands.

As the centuries passed, the island of Hirado continued its international connections when, even more shockingly, the Portuguese and the English arrived and set up their trading houses there during the Edo period in the early 17th century. These were later sent packing to the confines of nearby Dejima island by a nervous shogunate who feared the impact of these well-armed foreigners and their Christian God. Even more than that, they feared the influence they could have on the ambitions of the local feudal lords, who might have seized on the chance to avail themselves of the far more advanced foreign military technology on offer to mount a rebellion.

These days getting to the island, which boasted just a sleepy little fishing port with an aging population like most other parts of rural Japan, was a relatively simple affair, so long as you had a vehicle. All you had to do was drive across the picturesque Hirado Bridge from the mainland, which was naturally enough the pride of the island, and which could not but fail to remind any visiting American of the great Golden Gate Bridge spanning San Francisco Bay, only on a much smaller scale.

Today as the sun sparkled on the sea and the gulls circled slowly overhead as they had since time immemorial here, the large black SUV driven by the Odawara brothers roared across this same bridge, quickly crossing the narrow strait in less than a minute and headed at high speed onto the narrow road that led into the main part of town. Neither of its occupants was in the mood for taking in the view as they crossed the bridge, as they had express instructions from their superiors in Tokyo ringing in their ears that they were not to waste a minute in locating the man they had been sent to find.

They had now driven almost non-stop for fourteen hours from the capital, following the route that Jun had taken a few weeks earlier by trailing another car on a GPS device that had arrived a few hours before them and at almost the same speed. They were both exhausted, as they had stopped only briefly at the rest stations on the highways, and their last meal had been several hours earlier back in Osaka.

When they finally made it to their destination, just an old-fashioned village by the sea in which they both had no interest whatsoever, they quickly parked their car at the small car park near the only gas station and headed off to start making inquiries. Surely, they reasoned, someone in this little dump would know whom they were looking for, and this was indeed the case. However, whether or not those they asked were inclined to share that information was another question.

Jun, who had absolutely no inkling about the two men that had been sent to find him, and who genuinely believed that no one could have possibly followed him all the way down to this remote little town, had spent the morning innocently cleaning out a cluttered storeroom attached to the old family house, after which he had headed off to a small local supermarket to pick up a few things he needed for dinner.

After the shock of Professor Suzuki's passing, he had settled back into the easy rhythm of life here on the island remarkably quickly, just as he always had when his parents had taken him here every New Year and for the summer holidays, when he had enjoyed being spoilt by his grandparents and playing with his cousins, most of whom were the children of local fishermen and farmers, and who knew the island like the back of their hands.

In those far-off days, they had spent their time happily swimming off the local beaches and fishing from the pier, and quite often the older children were called on to help out on their relative's boats, which fished in the waters off the coast and where, if they had ventured far enough out on a clear day, you could even make out the shape of the island of Tsushima and the south-eastern part of the Korean peninsula, hazy in the sea mist.

It hadn't taken Jun very long to fall back into the laid-back lifestyle of the local people he had once been so familiar with as a child. Something about the place had made him slow down and relax after the horrors of the past few weeks, and now he spent his time going for long walks, sleeping late, and reacquainting himself with fishing. He had cleaned up the old fishing basket he had owned as a child and sometimes spent the afternoon at the pier or on a rocky outcrop off one of the beaches, where more often than not, he returned with dinner.

This morning as he walked down the road from his house, the men from the capital were busy putting questions to his rather suspicious neighbors, who, fortunately for Jun, were less than forthcoming with his address when confronted by these two rough-looking individuals with their suits and their Tokyo accents and their all too flashy black SUV. Most of the islanders took one look at them and decided that they had never heard of Jun Miyamoto, even though all of them knew him and his family as well as their own.

Jun did, however, take note of one man as he wandered down the road to the shops however, a stranger sitting on a bench at the port and staring out to sea. He seemed to be enjoying the view out over the little harbor, and taking a great interest in the fishing boats that were tied up along the pier. The man, who looked like he was in his late forties and was wearing an old tweed coat, had a long ponytail trailing down his back and was smoking what looked like a hand-rolled cigarette. Jun also noticed him because there was something about him that defined him as 'city' rather than someone from the countryside, and because it was unusual to see islanders just sitting around looking at the peaceful little bay like they had nothing to do. Here people worked with their hands for a living, either fishing or raising vegetables, and they didn't have the time to sit around loafing like that. That was something the tourists did, and there weren't many of them at this time of year.

Jun did his shopping at the little supermarket, which was run by one of his distant cousins, had a long chat about the health of his remaining family with the mother of one of his old friends who happened to be there as well, and finally managed to head home after more than an hour.

He walked back to his house the same way he had come with his heavy plastic shopping bags and a rucksack containing a large bag of rice, back past the little road that ran along the harbor, where he noticed that the man with the ponytail had vanished.

Probably just a tourist, he thought, as he knew most of the people around the island by face if not by their name, and he thought no more about it.

He trudged his way up the hill to his house, opened the front door, and headed into the kitchen with his bags. He was just about to put them on the kitchen counter when his senses prickled and he had a strange feeling that he was not alone.

"You need to pack a bag, Miyamoto-san. It's time to leave," said a soft voice just behind him.

He spun around and there, standing in the doorway to the kitchen behind him, was the man with the ponytail.

Before he could say a word, the man raised his hand as if asking for silence.

"I'm sorry to enter your house uninvited," the man said calmly, "but you are in considerable danger. I guess your old boss made you aware of that, didn't he? The fact that you could be in trouble? Otherwise, I guess you would not have hared off down here."

Jun glared at the man, but even though he was shocked to find this stranger standing in his kitchen, his instincts told him at the same time that he was not in any danger from him.

"Who the hell are you, and what are you doing in my house." he barked, nevertheless.

The man smiled and gave him a short bow of greeting.

"My name is Sal Nakamura. I was an acquaintance of Professor Suzuki, who asked me to make sure you were all right if anything happened to him. And the reason I am here… is that you are not all right. So… as I said, pack a bag and come with me. I reckon we have about ten minutes before the guys responsible for your boss's death walk in that door…"

Jun tried to protest, but Nakamura tapped his watch.

"Look, we don't have time to discuss this. We need to leave right now. Do you understand?"

Jun looked desperately around the kitchen and finally heaved a sigh.

"Give me a second, I need to find something important."

Sal nodded, and without a word went quickly up the stairs to one of the bedrooms that offered a view of the street outside, while Jun hurriedly threw some clothes and his laptop into an old duffel bag.

As Sal scanned the street, a few minutes later, and to his dismay, just as he had predicted, a large black SUV turned the nearest corner and started heading up the road to the house. He had watched the men arriving from his bench by the quay and had realized that the time available to them was much less than he had calculated.

A few seconds later the SUV was so close that he could clearly see the two men in suits sitting in the front.

He swore silently and ran downstairs again.

"Is there another way out of this house? Like a back way? I'm afraid we have even less time than I thought. We have company out front," he whispered to Jun, putting his finger to his lips to get the message across.

Jun picked up the duffel bag and zipped it shut.

"Follow me," he said quietly.

The two men went out into the garden at the rear of the house, where an old door that was almost impossible to see in the ivy-covered wall led them out into a tiny alley less than a meter wide that ran behind the houses.

"Excellent," said Sal. "Look, my car is down at the pier. Is there any way you can get us there without being seen?" he asked, glancing behind them.

Jun hesitated and thought for a moment. Finally, he nodded.

"You're lucky I grew up around here. Yeah…. there's a back way down to the water."

He gestured to Sal to follow him, and they moved quietly down the alley. However, they had not only gone more than a few steps when they heard a loud bang from inside the old house behind them.

"I think they've just kicked down your front door from the sound of that," said Sal as he pushed Jun ahead of him down the alley. They both broke into a run, and Jun led Nakamura unerringly through a maze of little pathways and tiny streets that only a local would have known. In less than two minutes they emerged from between some old shops onto the main road opposite the pier where

Sal's old black Toyota Harrier was parked, and a minute after that the journalist was gunning the car back across the Hirado bridge as fast as it could go.

"So... where are we going?" asked Jun looking out the back window of the car to see if anyone was following them, which fortunately they were not.

Sal smiled, and they made a sharp left off the bridge onto the first available road and then began to twist and turn around the lesser-known little roads that would eventually hook up with the main highway running north.

"We, my friend, are going to Nagano. I have a place there, and that's where my friend from the police is going to meet us. I think they've already been to my place in Tokyo, so that's too dangerous. Only a few people know about the other house, so we should be safe there."

"And what if we aren't? After all, those guys managed to find me down here... and I thought that was impossible, frankly," said Jun.

Sal nodded. "Fair point. We just have to be careful for a while. You have the flash drive?"

Jun started at his words.

"Maybe... why?" he said cautiously.

The other man smiled. "That's good to hear. And you have it with you? Excellent. Because we need to get it and you somewhere safe. Anyway, well done, you managed to survive so far. Old Suzuki was right to trust you."

Jun looked at the man and felt a sense of relief.

"You knew him?"

Sal nodded. "Briefly. He was friends with my uncle, and I was interested in his research, so we met a few times to discuss that. Maybe you knew of Professor Nakamura? He was a close associate of your old boss. Until he was murdered...."

Jun nodded. He remembered the old professor from his undergraduate days.

"He was murdered?"

"Yes. He and four of his friends. That's five. Six, if you count Suzuki. If I hadn't come along today, you would undoubtedly have had the pleasure of being number seven. I almost had that distinction myself, I think, back in Tokyo. Have you looked at the files?"

Jun shook his head.

"No. Suzuki asked me not to. He told me to get out of Tokyo, and then to hand the drive over to someone if something happened. To lay low, and not to look at the flash drive for my own safety. He even passworded it so that I wouldn't give in to temptation."

"And since you know it *has* a password, I presume you *did* try and have a look at it?" Sal smiled as he negotiated the entrance to the expressway heading to Tokyo and the main island of Honshu.

Jun looked out the window rather sheepishly. "Well... yes and no. I was just seeing if the files were OK. Anyway, I couldn't access it. As I said, he didn't give me the password."

"Well, that's actually good news for you. If you knew what was on it, you would be in even more trouble than you currently are," said Sal. "But that does rather present a problem, as I dunno the password either. Anyway, don't worry. We will be pretty safe if we can just get out of here and make it north without them catching up to us. We can let the police crypto guys figure it out."

Jun seemed to be calmer now and had stopped watching behind them.

"Well, that might not be necessary. You said your name is Sal Nakamura?"

Sal glanced over at him.

"That's me. Why?"

Jun looked at him and smiled for the first time.

"And you are a journalist?"

Sal passed him a little cardholder on the dashboard, and Jun took a business card from inside and inspected it.

"Happy now?" asked Sal.

Jun nodded. "I think so. Maybe you will be too.

"How come?"

Jun looked down at the business card.

"Because you are the guy he told me to give the flash drive to."

"Me?"

Jun nodded.

"What about the password, though," asked Sal.

Jun put the card in his shirt pocket.

"Six digits. Your uncle's birthday. Which I don't know, by the way."

Sal rolled his eyes. "Crafty old guy, Professor Suzuki. He seems to have been two steps ahead of both of us. To tell the truth, I don't know his birthday, but I sure as hell know someone who does…."

Chapter 16.

The Monastery at the End of Time

A cold autumn rain was falling as the four women passed through the main gate of the old Zen monastery. It lay at the end of a short path in the north-western part of Kyoto under the misty gaze of Mt. Hiei, the holy mountain that guarded the city against what the ancients believed were the inclement spirits of the North.

The rain did nothing whatsoever to detract from the stately atmosphere that seemed to clothe the old buildings under the dark green eminence of the mountain, but rather made it feel as if you had simply walked through some portal into another far more ancient time, and that you were not, in fact, just a few kilometers from the bustle of the modern city center.

Although Kenhou-ji was not a large monastery, and now only had thirty or so monks in residence, it had once been much more important as a training center for the Zen sect, and in its heyday many centuries ago had boasted over eight hundred clerics in residence as well as frequent visits and endowments from the aristocracy. However, the changing times had caused many of its lands to be sold off, and over the last three or four centuries, it had shrunk to its present size while still maintaining the most important of its buildings, some of which dated back to the Muromachi period some five hundred years earlier.

Apart from enjoying the favor of the aristocracy for many centuries, Kenhou-ji was also a- place where members of that class had been interred since the early eighth century, and, especially significant for the four friends visiting today, it was where many members from the disparate branches of the ruling Fujiwara family had found their rest. In addition, it was still overseen by an abbot who was himself a direct descendent of Teika no Fujiwara, and also where Teika's daughter, the Buddhist nun Ameka, had chosen to end her days almost fifty years after the death of her father. The monastery had thereafter remained in the keep of that branch of the Fujiwara family, and the position of abbot had been passed down through the generations to the present day.

As they sheltered for a moment under the gate, they took a moment to be part of the scene before them, like they had just been transported to a foreign land.

"This is such a lovely old place," said Sachie, who had been here before on previous trips for her research and knew the Abbot quite well. "I've been coming here since I was a student, and I never get tired of it."

Penelope and Fei nodded in agreement, and Professor Xu gave a sigh.

"You know, every time I come to Kyoto, and I probably shouldn't say this, but particularly when you are in my line of academia, I can't help but think about how much we lost in China... you know, especially during the Cultural

Revolution. So many thousands of places like this were destroyed. And all for what, I wonder."

"Politics, I guess," said Fei. "I think that's why my grandparents got out and came to Japan. They were both devout Taoists, and their temples were also destroyed by the Red Guards. Out with the old... as they used to say...."

Xu nodded. "People just don't understand what a fragile thing the past is. It's always just slipping away, like sand through your fingers. You have to fight to keep any of it, love it, and value it. But then in some countries... there are times that doesn't happen, and then one day you wake up... and it's gone. My father had plenty to say about those days when he was alive... but just to us family. Even as a historian, he couldn't even whisper what he really thought, or his career would have simply ended. It's absurd, but any serious discussion of Mao's excesses is still kept quiet. And you know what they say about a people that don't learn history...At least here though..." she opened her arms as if to embrace the ancient place, "Here it's all still gloriously alive."

"Very much so, as we may be about to find out," said Penelope as they watched a young man in a black priest's *koromo* come clattering towards them in his traditional wooden *geta* clogs from the direction of the main hall.

The young man bowed politely, and told them that the abbot was expecting them.

"Please follow me, and I'll take you to him. Getting lost around here is easy if you don't know your way. It's a lot bigger than it looks..." he explained pleasantly as he led the way through the buildings to the abbot's residence, an old wooden house surrounded by a small walled garden tucked away behind the main hall.

"Have you been here long?" asked Fei as they walked, and the young man smiled modestly. "No, this is my first year. I graduated from Komozawa university in Tokyo and was at another monastery before I was ordained. Do you know Komozawa? You sound a bit like you are from Tokyo…."

"Komozawa? Oh yes, it's very famous," said Penelope, who knew the Buddhist university well.

Sachie touched Penelope on the arm as they waited for the abbot to greet them.

"Let me know if the abbot reminds you of anyone in particular," she whispered somewhat mysteriously. Penelope raised an eyebrow and waited to see what she meant.

The young monk opened a door in the wall surrounding the little house, and they heard a bell tinkling inside as they stepped into the little formal garden.

A few moments later, the front door opened, and a rather frail-looking elderly man in black robes and wearing a mustard-colored *rakusu* around his neck came out to greet them, and Penelope's eyes opened wide as she grasped what Sachie had meant.

Except for the fact that he had a shaven head, the abbot bore an almost uncanny resemblance to the former Heisei emperor Akihito, the father of the present Emperor Reiwa. Penelope glanced at Fei and Xu, and wondered if they all shared the same epiphany.

The abbot gave them a low bow, and Sachie introduced them.

"So nice of you to make the journey here. And from... Kamakura, was it? One of my favorite cities. I haven't been there for years and years, though... age, you know. I find it hard just to get around Kyoto as I used to these days. Anyway, please come in and have some tea. So nice to see you again, Okutani-san. It's been a long time," said the abbot, who clearly enjoyed chatting.

The young monk disappeared inside ahead of them, and the abbot showed them into an elegant little tatami mat room he used for visitors, which had a highly polished low table surrounded by five cushions. The women settled themselves on their *zabuton* and, looking around them, the first thing to catch the eye was in the alcove, where there was a beautiful hanging scroll with a painting of Mt. Hiei in the mist, very much like it was today, which Penelope at once recognized was by the famous Zen artist Sesshu. In front of this was a small branch with some dazzling red and gold maple leaves extending from an elegant old ceramic vase of Bizen pottery from Okayama prefecture.

"That's such a beautiful painting," Penelope commented, and the abbot turned and glanced at it.

"One of our treasures. And one of the advantages of being in the same place for about twelve hundred years. You tend to collect things... Some people say I'm of a similar age... and some days when it rains, I have to agree," he smiled. "It plays havoc with my knees. I even have to do my meditation using a chair these days. I'm not sure the Zen patriarchs would have ever tolerated such luxuries...."

"If you are worried about setting a bad example, please don't be silly. I know they all love you here..." said Sachie with a smile.

The abbot laughed, and at that moment the door slid open, and the young monk returned with a tray of hot tea in beautiful green ceramic cups, which he distributed around the table along with some little plates of dried sweets.

They chatted for a while about Sachie's various books, some of which the abbot had read, and about the monastery, where he had been abbot for the last forty or more years.

"You know, I hate to be rude," said Fei interrupting his discourse. "But you really do have a resemblance to... well, maybe other people have mentioned it?"

The abbot smiled. "Oh, don't worry. People have been saying that to me since I was in my twenties and he was just the crown prince. I guess one shouldn't be surprised. I mean... he is a, well, distant relative. You know all the Fujiwara's have the same kind of look... and we are both about the same age too...."

They all laughed, and the abbot rang a little bell and asked the monk who answered it to bring them some more tea.

"You know, abbot, we have a question to ask you about another of your relatives, if you don't mind. We were hoping you might be able to shed some light on something," said Sachie.

"Ah yes. You mentioned it in your email. Such a convenient thing, email. I'm quite proud to say I've even mastered using it myself... so there is still hope for the elderly, I guess, even in places like this," he smiled. "About

Ameka? Yes, I remember now. What would you like to know?"

"Well, we've been doing some research into her. Apparently, she came here to seek refuge the year after Teika died. I think it was in 1242?"

"Yes, that's right. You do know your history well. And as you maybe also know, here in Kyoto that was just last week. The locals tend to think like that here…" he smiled.

"And she stayed here the rest of her life?"

"Yes. In those days, you see, there was a nunnery attached to the monastery. It was a lot bigger back then. We had a number of sub-temples too, on Mt. Hiei and other places. She later also became Abbess, which was, of course, extremely common for people of her rank. In her day the nunnery was quite large too, there were a few hundred of them back then."

"So, she's buried here?" asked Xu.

The abbot nodded. "Oh yes. I can have them show you her grave on the way out if you like. It's not far from the main gate…."

"Actually, what we were wondering… are there any… artifacts… you know, from her days here?"

The abbot looked up innocently.

"Artifacts? I'm not sure what you mean; I'm afraid… we have a lot of historical documents and other things here. Not so much from that period, though. We've sent a lot of it to museums and universities over the last fifty years or so, it just wasn't a good idea to store it all here. And people want to see it too, so… not so much left here these days."

Xu opened her briefcase and passed him a photocopy of a very ancient-looking document.

The abbot put on his reading glasses and gave a little chuckle.

"Oh… this… Yes, yes. I recognize *that* handwriting. Although there are so many forgeries floating around these days, you wouldn't believe what they got up to in the past. Perhaps you know all about that. This what they call, what is it… the Teika thing… The document they found, when was it… about thirty years ago now?"

Penelope nodded. "Yes. The very one. Historians like Professor Xu here call it the Teika Fragment. So, you're familiar with it?"

The abbot stared at the document for a while.

"Yes, I've seen it before. I believe it was found in a private collection somewhere. Wasn't that the story? Inserted in some other book?"

Professor Xu nodded. "Yes, that's right. It was found using an X-ray. It had been glued underneath another page. Pretty common practice back then when paper was an expensive commodity."

"Ah, yes. Strange how we always value things more when we take the time to make them by hand. I think the world has largely forgotten that…." said the abbot with a sigh. 'Anyway, please tell me what my esteemed ancestor has scribbled that you think is so important." He pushed his glasses back up his long nose, and once again, Penelope was struck by the resemblance to his more famous relative.

"According to this letter, at least we think it's part of a letter, Teika was planning to write a history of the imperial line. Like the *Shiji* in China. Are you familiar with that?" asked Xu.

"So I gather. Unfortunately, he never seemed to have gotten around to it. Is that right?"

Sachie nodded. "That appears to be the case. I guess we'll never know. I suppose it could turn up somewhere though. Hidden away…."

"That's true, you never know," said the abbot. "You know, just a few years ago, they found an almost completely original text of Basho's *Oku no hoso michi* somewhere in Kyoto… incredible find…."

Professor Xu nodded. "So, if you have read this, you know something else is mentioned. The thing that Teika says he was going to use as a base for his history. And the thing is… we are sure it existed. I'm talking about what he calls the Jade Scroll. It was a text written on strips of jade that dates from the very earliest times. I think we are talking about over 400 BC, long before we have any other histories of the imperial line. Back in what they call the period of the legendary emperors."

The abbot was quiet for a moment and looked around him at the four women.

"Why do you think this artifact exists?" he asked.

Sachie spoke up. "Well, Teika would hardly have mentioned it as part of his threat to write the history if it hadn't. And that threat was taken seriously, so its existence must have been known to the court and Emperor Go-Toda at the time. So yes, we are sure it existed…."

The abbot nodded slowly. "I see. I guess that would make sense. And it would be exciting, I'm sure. Would you like some more tea?" he asked, picking up the small green teapot.

The four women looked at each other, as the abbot looked for all the world like he wanted to change the subject.

"Actually, as an expert on the family, we were wondering what *you* think happened to it?" Fei rather too pointedly.

The abbot put down the teapot and wiped his glasses with a small cloth he took from the sleeve of his robes.

"Well… I'm sure I've no idea. After all, I'm no historian. I leave all that to people like Okutani-san here… and of course you, professor," he said with a smile and looked at Xu.

There was a short silence, and then Sachie spoke.

"If you don't mind, abbot, I was wondering if we could run a theory past you. Just to get your view…. You see, we think Teika entrusted it to his daughter, Ameka. Her name was Shuka when she lived here. A word that means 'guardian,' I believe… And we think she brought it here."

=====================

An hour later the young monk led them back towards the main gate.

"The abbot said you were interested in seeing a grave? The grave of Teika no Fujiwara's daughter, Ameka? It's just over here…" he gestured to a little pathway and led them to the main graveyard attached to the monastery, where he stopped in front of a simple little flat stone with a very old stone lantern. A small vase for flowers was placed in front of it, and a little metal plaque describing the famous occupant.

They stood for a minute in the drizzling rain under their umbrellas.

"So… this is her…" said Penelope sadly.

"Yes… Shuka. Her Buddhist name. She lived here for almost fifty years," said the young monk.

A few minutes later, he escorted them back to the main gate, where he gave them a low bow of farewell, and then turned back to the main hall and left them.

"Well, that went well," said Fei, as the four women walked back through the rainy backstreets towards Kyoto station.

Penelope smiled. "Hmmm… Well, he didn't deny it, did he?"

They all knew that the meeting seemed to have disturbed the elderly abbot, but they were not sure exactly why. He had not given any direct response to their idea about the Scroll, but merely shrugged and told them it was an interesting idea, and that he wondered what must have become of it.

"You know, it was his first reaction that interested me," said Xu. "Did you notice he didn't say he'd never heard of it being there? He just said that no one had ever mentioned it before. I found that very interesting."

"I agree," said Penelope. "I noticed that too. That's like when somebody asks you if you have eaten their last piece of cake, and the immediate answer isn't "not me."

"Odd, I thought," said Sachie. "And then we all got pretty quickly booted out. I thought that was strange too. It's not like he gets many inquiries about it… like he said."

"Maybe he just thought we were wasting his time," said Fei nonchalantly. "It could be just that, you know."

"What I would like to know is, why wouldn't he want to do the country a favor and put it in a museum if he has it? I mean, the thing is priceless," said Xu.

"Maybe. But maybe it's priceless for the wrong reasons," said Penelope quietly, and the other women turned to look strangely at her as they walked.

"Meaning?" asked Fei.

Penny stopped in the middle of the footpath and looked at them.

"Meaning, we know that the Scroll challenges the standard story about the imperial line, perhaps because it doesn't support the usual nonsense about the first emperor Jimmu being descended from the Sun God and all that. Of course, this is not all that bad, as no one but the ultra-right believes it. It's what else it might say that may be a cause of consternation. What I can't figure out though is why, if he has it or knows about it, he isn't telling us. Doesn't he understand that people have been killed over it?"

They were all quiet for a moment, and then Professor Xu spoke quietly.

"Perhaps you have to make him understand, Penny-*sensei*."

Penelope nodded grimly. "Perhaps you're right."

Chapter 17.

The Return of the Court

Chief Inspector Yamashita opened the blinds to his office and the morning sun poured in, causing him to swear and shield his eyes. He looked back at his normally tidy office and the blanket lying on the end of the couch where he had slept for the last three nights, shook his head, stretched, and gave a loud sigh. He was, however, not the only one in the station who had given up the comforts of home over the last week.

For the last several days he had assembled and led a small task force of officers, mostly from the local force, but he had also drawn in several leading experts on Japanese politics, including journalists from some of the major papers like Sal Nakamura, in order to get to the bottom of why anyone would want to kill a bunch of archaeologists over the last twenty years. However, he found what they had come up with so far hard to fathom, a feeling that anyone who starts turning over the rocks of the ultra-right in any country is somewhat bound to share.

There was a knock on the door, and the unshaven face of Detective Sergeant Yokota came into sight around it.

"They're ready for you, sir," he said in a tired voice. "I must admit it's kind of nice of them to all get together at this hour…."

Yamashita nodded and gave a weak smile.

"I guess they just want to get to the bottom of this too. Any word from Sal, by the way?"

Yokota shook his head. "Not since they got out of Nagasaki prefecture. If they're headed up here they would have arrived by now. I dunno how he found that guy, but I wish he'd left it to us to go and get him. We could have used the local boys to pick him up…."

Yamashita sighed again.

"Don't get me started on the wily ways of Sal Nakamura. That man would do anything to get the story first. Don't worry, I'm going to have a word with him, believe me."

"Do you think they're safe, sir?"

Yamashita shrugged. "I hope so. Sal's pretty good at covering his tracks. What I want to know is how the other lot got down there so fast. It seems to have been some kind of a race to get to him…."

Yokota slouched his heavy body against the door frame and scratched his cheek. "That's what I'm wondering too, sir. There's something not right about the whole thing…."

"Well, we'll find out. Anyway, let's go and see what the others have turned up."

He picked up his mug of coffee, and they walked upstairs to the conference room where a female officer and her colleague were busy setting up the meeting, which was to be held by video conference, as so many of their meetings had been since the pandemic. Yamashita had privately found this practice to have been a huge time saver though, and he had greatly appreciated the shift to online meetings, overcoming years of reluctance by the usually technophobic police force who still believed the only way to solve any crime was face-to-face meetings accompanied by filling out an ocean of paperwork.

He took his seat in the conference room, and while the other officers took their seats beside him, several faces appeared on the screen, representing the eclectic little network of experts in organized crime and politics that Yamashita and Yokota had painstakingly put together and been working with over the last week.

"So, ladies and gentlemen, thanks so much for turning up at ... 8am... I know that's a bit early for most of you...." said Yokota, looking up at the screen. "Perhaps you could bring the Chief Inspector up to date with what you've been able to turn up since our last meeting?"

There was silence for a few seconds, and then one of the reporters, an older man called Akimoto, who was a respected correspondent for the leading Asahi Newspaper group spoke up.

"Good morning, all. I've been doing a bit of digging, and I've asked one of my younger associates here to join us. He's a bit of an expert on the *uyoku*, the ultra-right. He's been following them for years, and last year after the assassination of Shinzo Abe he published a series of articles on them."

The younger man, dressed in a polo shirt and sporting shoulder-length hair and a goatee waved at them in a friendly manner from another window on the screen and introduced himself.

"Kensuke Yamada. I'm also with the *Asahi*," he said briefly.

Yamashita and Yokota welcomed him, and Yamashita told him he had read some of his work. Since the assassination of the former prime minister by a disgruntled former Self-Defense operative whose family had donated their entire net worth to a Korean-based 'Christian' cult that the ruling party, and the Abe family particularly, had encouraged close ties with for several decades in exchange for support and donations, there had been a decided uptick in the interest of both the media and law enforcement in the activities of fringe groups, whether they were religious or political. The death of the former Prime Minister had been a major wake-up call, if one were needed, that these groups were a serious threat to public order and needed to be better monitored and understood.

Yamada began to describe the research he had been asked to do by his more senior colleague.

"Akimoto-san said you were interested in finding out a bit more about the *Shinenkai*, the *New Flame Society*?"

Yamashita and Yokota both nodded.

"Yes, we would be very interested in whatever you know. They've come across our radar lately, in connection not only with the killing of Professor Suzuki but perhaps also with the death of several of his colleagues over the years…." said Yamashita.

Yamada said he understood.

"They are a pretty misunderstood group, I think," he said.

"Misunderstood? In what way?" asked Yokota.

Yamada paused.

"Well, I guess I mean 'misunderstood' in terms of how the public, and also a lot of their members, perceive it. Let me give you a bit of background...." The reporter cleared his throat and shuffled some papers on his desk.

"The group has actually been around for more than forty years. It was started by a bunch of old ruling party diehards with family connections to a number of convicted war criminals, you know, like Abe's family. This never stopped them from gaining access to the top tier of ruling party politics, and the group has been slowly but surely gathering members over the years. As you know, the ruling party is split into several factions, but this group is sort of a meta-faction, and has members from across all the big, leading groups that make up the ruling party, and also the opposition parties. Now, this is what I mean by *misunderstood*...."

He paused for a moment and took a sip of water from a plastic bottle in front of him.

"What I mean is, if you are a member of this group and look at its normal activities, it's usually totally harmless. They are basically a conservative and right-wing *Shinto* group. So they support things like traditional Japanese family values, the observance of Shinto rights, and the veneration of the war dead at places like the Yasukuni shrine in Tokyo. The latter is controversial as you know because it enshrines a couple of dozen Class A war criminals, so that pisses off the Koreans and Chinese whenever people visit, and of course, they dislike anything 'foreign', which they see as corrupting Japanese morals. Anyway, so far, so harmless. There is nothing they support which a lot of people in Japan would have any problem with. That, naturally enough, is why the ruling party has been the ruling party since the end of the war…" he smiled. "You guys with me so far?" he asked.

Yokota and Yamashita nodded.

"Still waiting for the bit about why they are so 'misunderstood'?" asked Yokota pleasantly, hoping the young reporter would get to the point.

"Right. Yes, well… they are 'misunderstood' in the sense that despite everything I have just said, there seems to be more to them than just that."

"In what sense?" asked Yamashita.

"Well, what I am about to tell you is all speculation and rumor, but here goes… in the sense that this group has an inner core and an outer core, just like an onion. The outer core, that's ninety-nine-point-nine percent of the members, has no real problem with it, especially if you like all that conservative rhetoric and stuff. But rumors have been circulating for years that there is a very, very centralized hard-core of leaders with a much more reactionary agenda. And *they* are prepared to go to some lengths to ensure it gets enacted."

Yamashita and Yokota looked at each other.

"I think I have heard this story before, but please proceed. What kind of agenda?" asked the chief inspector.

Yamada paused.

"Well, it's kind of obvious in a way. They want the restoration of imperial rule."

There was dead silence for a moment before Yuichi Imabara, a senior detective from Tokyo, spoke up.

"Sorry? They want *what*?" he asked in a confused tone.

"Maybe I'm not being clear, sorry." said the young reporter. "Basically, they want to replace parliament with a court. The emperor makes all the decisions, supported by a group of nobles. Think Heian period, you know, a thousand years ago."

"You're kidding, right?" said Imabara.

Yamada shook his head. "I'm not. That's what these guys believe. As far as they are concerned, the current situation is just for gathering support until they can achieve their goals."

Yokota leaned forward.

"Are you talking about a possible coup? Against the government?"

Yamada nodded. "Maybe, in the end. If it came to that. But only with the support of the military and a good number of important politicians, which, of course, they don't have and probably never would have. They would be the first to admit that they are still a long way from their goals at this point. They want to see this come about peacefully, at least at the moment that's the M.O.…"

The police in the room now had their ears up.

"Is this something we should be worried about?" asked Yamashita in a concerned tone.

Yamada shook his head. "Not at this point, no. But it's definitely something you should all be aware of. That's all I'm saying."

Yamashita sat back in his chair.

"OK, so tell us… how does this group relate to our case? I mean, what's it got to do with these murdered historians?"

Akimoto, the younger man's senior, now spoke.

"Maybe I can help you there. You see, as my young colleague here was explaining, the big thing with this group is the person of the Japanese emperor. They still regard him like he was styled in the old Meiji constitution before the war, as a 'sacred' being. So, if anything is going to make this group turn violent, it is any public disrespect shown to him. This has been a thing with the ultra-right groups since before the war. 'Protect the emperor. Expel the barbarians', all that stuff, as the old Meiji slogan went. So what I'm wondering is if this group of archaeologists happened across something that in some way cast doubt on what you might call the 'imperial story.' The accepted history of the imperial family. That would make them all hopping mad, for sure."

"Sorry," said Imabara, I don't follow you. What do you mean by 'the imperial story'?

"The story of the bloodline, that's probably the most important aspect, I guess. The belief that the Japanese imperial family has an *unbroken* bloodline, stretching all the way back to the first emperor, Jimmu. Even though he was 'legendary,' meaning there is not a shred of evidence he existed. Of course, as far as the far-right is concerned, he was descended from the Shinto sun god, thus 'sacred' as the old Meiji constitution said. 'Sacred Japan' should be ruled by a divine emperor. It's a very simple creed, and it was official policy in the military period before the war. That's what the hard-core want to get back to."

"And these murdered men?"

"Well, if you are saying the far-right murdered them, I would presume it was because they disrespected this 'story.' Would that be accurate? Like you say, they were archaeologists, right? Did they go anywhere near a royal tomb?"

The question lay on the ground before the group like an unexploded bomb.

"Would that be a serious problem?"

Both of the journalists nodded vehemently.

"That would be *the* most serious problem. And also a violation of the law, as you know. Those tombs are sacrosanct. They've never been open to study. Ever. And the government and the far-right especially want to keep it that way," said Akimoto.

"Why would they want to do that, though? Aren't they important for historical research?" said Imabara.

The two reporters both smiled.

"Well, the official line is that it would be 'disrespectful,' you know, considering they are Japanese emperors. Bordering on the profane. But…"

"But what?" said Yokota.

The younger reporter answered. "I think obviously the real reason is that they're scared of what they might find. You know, something that contradicts the 'story' of the bloodline. I mean, what if there is DNA there that disproves it? Or even worse, that the diseased wasn't even Japanese? Or something even worse?"

"What, like they are American?" joked Yokota, earning a disapproving look from his boss. The reporters both laughed, however.

"Well, that would be interesting, I guess," said Yamada. "The point is, though, they have never been opened, and as far as the far-right is concerned it's just about protecting imperial dignity. If there *were* another reason, that would also make much more sense."

"OK," said Yamashita, "we can get back to this later, though. What do you know about the *Shinenkai* group now? I mean, who's really in charge of it?"

"That's an interesting question, actually. The nominal head of the group is one Katayama Yasunori. At least on paper," said Yamada.

"You mean this guy? Just a minute." Yokota quickly found the file he was looking for on the laptop in front of him and shared the picture of Katayama from the *Odawara Iaido Dojo* homepage, the same one they had shown to the younger Odawara brother on their trip to the *dojo* the previous week.

Yamada and Akimoto both nodded. "Yes, that's him. Where did you find it? That looks like a *kendo* club or something?" said Yamada.

"*Iaido* club," said Yamashita. "One with lots of right-wing members, one of whom killed the late Professor Suzuki."

Akimoto and Yamada both nodded.

"That's very interesting, actually. There's been rumors for a while about something like that… I'm not surprised you managed to find a link."

"Rumors about what?" said Imabara, leaning forward into his screen.

"Well, just a rumor, but that the *Shinenkai* had some kind of secret enforcement arm. Something connected with right-wing students and maybe also to organized crime. There's been talk, especially on the far-right internet chat rooms, that the only way to really get what they want in the end is to embrace violent revolution. Co-opt the military. That sort of thing."

Yamashita raised an eyebrow. "You mean like in the Mishima Incident?"

"Yeah, sure. It bears a resemblance to Hitler's Beer Hall putsch in Munich in the 1920s. Violent, but it all came to nothing at the time. At least, that's how it's viewed by the far-right. They learned from that. The next one they intend to be a lot more successful...."

"Wow. I can't believe I'm hearing this," said Imabara.

"Believe it," said Yamada. "I can direct you to a dozen internet chat rooms where you can read far worse ideas than that one. But anyway, as to who is really in charge... just give me a moment."

They all waited while the reporter looked something up, and then the face of another elderly man dressed in black *kimono* and a *hakama* pleated skirt flashed up on the screen.

"That's a familiar face," said Yamashita. "I think I've seen him somewhere...."

The older journalist nodded.

"Meet Masakichi Bando. Otherwise known by his political nickname, the *kuromaku*, or 'Puppet Master.' 'The String-puller.' Whatever you like."

Yokota leaned forward and peered at the picture. "Never heard of him," he muttered.

"Doesn't surprise me. He's a bit before your time," said Akimoto with a smile. "He was pretty well-known at one time."

Yamashita nodded.

"Wasn't he a minister or something a long time ago?"

"Yep, that's him. Minister for Justice, actually, in the old Fujiyama government. You may remember that the Justice ministry is also in charge of immigration, and old Bando-*sensei* crafted some pretty draconian regulations at the time to keep foreigners and foreign businesses out of Japan. One of his pet themes, it appears."

"Anti-foreigner? Makes sense, I guess," said Yokota.

"Anyway," said Yamada, "He's the real deal as far as the *Shinenkai* go. His friend Katayama, also a former minister for Sport, funnily enough, is the face of the group, but he takes his orders from Bando, who is *far* more influential in the factional politics of the ruling party. He's only been in the cabinet once himself, but he wields considerable power through *Shinenkai*, which more than half the party and all the cabinet belong to these days. And he's far more hard-line than the group he runs usually portrays itself as."

"So, in your opinion," asked Yamashita, "Do you think he could orchestrate some kind of violence?"

"Word is… yes. If those sword guys are associated with him, that could be the rumored link to various people 'disappearing' over the years. They sound right up his alley."

"It does rather, doesn't it…" said Yamashita dryly. "OK. Let us get back to you all. It looks like we have a bit more investigating to do…."

Chapter 18

The Feint

Twenty-four hours after the video conference with the reporters, things had changed rapidly for the worse.

Chief Inspector Yamashita and his detective sergeant were now standing outside a little cottage down a sideroad in a remote village in Nagano prefecture surrounded by a vast pine forest about a hundred and fifty kilometers from the capital. Several other police vehicles were there with them, their flashing lights lighting up the trees in a display of law enforcement never before seen by the few curious locals that lived nearby.

Two old ladies who lived near the turnoff for the cottage near the tiny village of Kami-Ochiai had wandered up the little forestry road and were now staring in disbelief as ever more police vehicles roared past them towards the little house in the trees.

"That's where that nice chap from Kamakura used to stay," one said.

"The one with the ponytail? Whose sister was an actress?" asked her friend.

"Yes, that's the one, although you almost never saw her. He used to come up here by himself, mainly…."

The other woman stared suspiciously down the little dirt road toward the house.

"I wonder what he's done..." she said in a quite unnecessary whisper.

Chief Inspector Yamashita, for his part, was sitting glumly on a sawn-off tree stump with an axe leaning against it that seemed to point to its use as a chopping block for firewood in front of the cottage when one of the forensic technicians came up to him holding a small round metallic object in a plastic evidence bag.

"This what you were looking for, sir?" said the tech, a young man in the standard white plastic suit that all the forensic people wore when collecting evidence.

Yamashita took one look at it and swore bitterly under his breath.

"Where was it?"

"Like you said. Under the back bumper of the car. The usual spot for these things. No one ever looks there."

Yokota came up carrying a clipboard, and his boss passed him the bag.

"GPS tracker?" he asked.

His boss nodded.

"Ten dollars from Amazon these days," he opined. "Everything the modern criminal needs, delivered to your door...."

His boss gave him a rueful stare. "I'm such a bloody idiot, Yokota. Think about it. How did they suddenly arrive in Nagasaki only a few hours after Sal? We should have been here to meet them... too late now," he said with a frown.

The chief inspector stood up, retrieved the bag from Yokota, and handed it back to the tech.

"Sal *told* me they'd been following him around Kamakura. He even sent me an email with a picture of their car. Stolen license plates, of course. I sent a couple of boys out to his house when I got his mail, but they were gone. They must have put this on his car and then just waited to see where he went. They knew he was connected with Suzuki and that he'd been looking into that and his uncle's killing. I guess they thought that he would eventually lead them to wherever Suzuki's research assistant was. And you know? They were dead right. He managed to give them the slip in Nagasaki after meeting up with Miyamoto, but they knew exactly where he was going...."

"And now?"

Yokota gestured at the house, which they had found thoroughly ransacked by the time they had arrived.

"And now they have them, and they will soon have the only copy of Suzuki's research. And then God knows what will happen to them."

Yamashita stood and swore loudly again, and the tech returned to his examination of Sal's car.

Sal had called Yamashita earlier that day and informed him that he was on his way to the cottage with Miyamoto, and briefly related the narrow escape they had in Nagasaki. However, by the time the two police officers made it to Nagano to meet with them, it had been too late, and they had arrived to find the old cottage turned upside-down and the two men gone. Sal's car with their phones and other possessions had been found parked outside, but it too had been ransacked and the contents scattered on the ground around it.

The two men were silent for a while, and watched the forensic technicians going in and out of the cottage, documenting its contents and searching for anything that might help in the search that was being mounted for Sal and Miyamoto.

Eventually, Yamashita rose to his feet with a look of determination.

"Sir?" asked Yokota.

The chief inspector looked around to check they were not being overheard, and whispered quietly to Yokota.

"Are we still on?

"Yes, sir. So far, so good. They are at the home… The local boys just confirmed it."

"Who do you have on them?"

"Yamazaki, sir. We went to the academy together. You can trust him."

"OK. Tell him not to get too close. If he spooks them before we are ready, this will turn out badly. Anyway, it's time to bring them in. All of them. Shove them in separate interrogation rooms. Make them wait until I get there."

"Yes, sir. It'll be a pleasure. What do you want me to do with them?"

"For the moment, nothing. Let's make them sweat a bit. And then, we are going to squeeze them until the pips scream…" his boss said grimly. "First up, there is someone I need to see. And by the way, Yokota. I hope you were not counting on a pension out of this job. If this thing goes south, you and I will both be looking for something else to do…."

"Worry about that when it happens, sir," said Yokota with a nonchalant air.

The chief inspector gave him a nod, and they both headed for their car to begin the trip back to Kamakura.

====================

Since his cousin Hisafumi's suicide while in detention, Keiichi had made a habit of checking in on his aunt at his mother's request, just to make sure she was still OK. His own father had been to his brother's house on several occasions since the death as well, but Keiichi never accompanied him if it was at all possible. Although his father was a rough and fairly uncouth individual, he was not an innately violent man, and kept his fighting to the *dojo*, where he did the lion's share of the teaching.

His uncle Yasuhiro, a huge, brooding man with a bald pate, small pig-like eyes and a thick black beard, was a completely different person, though. Both he and his late son had famously evil tempers, would fly into uncontrollable rages, and were the most hard-line of all the members of the group of right-wing fanatics that they associated with both online and in person. As a child, Keiichi had been on the receiving end of his uncle's violence on several occasions, and now did his best to avoid contact with him. You never knew what kind of mood he was going to be in, and he certainly maintained a reign of terror over both his family and the other students at the *dojo*, who were all rightly scared to death of him. He had also, like his own father, been in prison after the Mishima Incident when they were students, but he had also been imprisoned on two subsequent occasions for vicious assaults at anti-government demonstrations, and those were only the more obvious crimes the police had been able to pin on him.

His aunt Chinami was not at all like her husband, however. A slender and gentle woman, always dressed in an elegant kimono and, like his own mother Meiko, completely in awe of her husband and someone who would not have dared speak out against the brother's beliefs nor any of their actions.

Such was the family Keiichi and his cousin had grown up in, and that was why he fully understood why Hisafumi had acted as he had. The boy had grown up to be a peerless martial artist, very much like him, but he had also been completely under the thumb of his father, whom he hero-worshipped and had always been desperate to please.

The cousins had both idolized and been terrified of their fathers in equal measure growing up and had understood from their very earliest childhoods that their role in life was to obey without question any command they were given, something which had made them the butt of many jokes in their high school, where they were surrounded by other youths who never spoke to either of their parents and didn't even know what their father or mother did for a living.

Given the terrible events of the last few weeks, Keiichi's mother had been very worried about her sister-in-law, who was probably her closest friend, and well understood the toll her son's death had taken on her, even if Chinami herself had found it impossible to say anything or to express her feelings to her husband at home. A large picture of Hisafumi adorned the family altar in their living room, draped with the appropriate black ribband, and as far as his father, the rest of the family, and the political group they were a part of believed, he was a hero and a martyr for the cause and an honor to their family. That was all that needed to be said about it, and tears were a sign of weakness and regret that could not be tolerated.

In Keiichi's own home though, the death of his cousin had been met with a quiet yet unrestricted grief, and both his father and mother, although they understood the reason for his actions, had taken his death hard. But the bond between the brothers was unshakable, and Keiichi knew that his father would never challenge his older brother on any action or plan that the latter had decided upon.

That morning, after his usual solitary morning practice at the family *dojo,* he had returned to find his uncle Yasuhiro and his father breakfasting together in the living room where they were being carefully served by his mother. After this meal, they had announced that they had 'a meeting with someone important' in Nagatacho, the political heart of Tokyo, and that they would be back later in time for the afternoon classes. Keiichi knew they often had meetings with people in Nagatacho, although the contents of these meetings and who they were with were never divulged. It was always implied that they were concerning 'the cause', although what that actually meant was somewhat amorphous.

After they left, Mieko found her son in his room.

"Do you think you could drop in on your aunt this morning while they are out? I just wanted to hear how she is… you know," she said as she stood obsequiously in the doorway to her son's room.

Keiichi had agreed and told her he would pop in and see her on his way to university, and she had given him a bag of winter oranges to take with him as a gift.

His uncle and his wife lived about a kilometer away on the way to the local train station, and it had only taken Keiichi a few minutes out of his way to get to their place, which was an old-fashioned wooden house much like his own, only theirs had a closed garage to the side where his uncle parked the black Toyota SUV he had acquired recently.

Keiichi knocked on the door, and his aunt opened it a second or two later, dressed in her usual kimono over which, like a lot of housewives, she wore a long white apron. She was still a pretty woman with a lovely small face, and she also still wore her hair long in a style that was more common with younger, single women than people of her age. Keiichi had always liked his aunt, and if he admitted the truth, he had always had a slight crush on her, despite the gap in their ages. His aunt had always been extremely kind to him growing up, and a more or less constant presence in his life, both consoling and motherly.

Today though, and knowing her well, he could at once sense that there was something not right in the house.

"Kei-chan! What are you doing here?" she exclaimed, nervously looking back into the interior of the house in such a way that the boy got the distinct impression there was something back there that she didn't want him to see.

Keiichi bowed politely and held out the bag of oranges.

"Mother asked me to drop these around to you and to ask how you were doing," he said, looking over her shoulder to see what she was attempting to hide.

"Oh, that's very kind of her. And you. Thank you. She needn't have bothered, though. I'm fine. Please tell her that."

Keiichi nodded. "OK, I'll do that. I think father is out today with uncle, so I'm sure you could pop round for tea if you wanted…" he said.

His words seemed to have a troubling effect on his aunt which he found strange, as he knew full well the women often got together secretly for a gossip when their husbands were away for the day.

"Oh… no. Please tell her I can't today. I have to… well… I have to stay here. Your uncle asked me to… specifically… so…."

Once again, she stared back over her shoulder at something to the rear of the house.

Keiichi told her not to worry, and that he was just popping by on his way to university now, but he also got the strong feeling that his aunt seemed eager to close the door and see him on his way. He bowed again, said his farewells, and headed back out the little gate to where his bicycle was waiting for him.

As he put his foot on the pedal though, something made him pause. He thought about just cycling off, but his aunt's behavior left him perplexed. He was not a naturally curious youth, but this time, for some unknown reason, he decided to take a quick look at the rear of the house, just to put his mind to rest. He parked his bicycle on its stand again and quietly opened the front gate. This time he walked around the corner of the house onto a narrow little path barely as wide as he was, that took him past the little bathroom window to the rear where there was a small back garden with an old wooden tool shed in the corner.

The garden looked as it always did, and he stood there momentarily wondering what to do. If he was spotted he knew his uncle would be furious, as the older man detested 'snooping', as he often called it and trusted no one. His aunt might also wonder what he was up to, and he was loathe to make her think worse of him.

The tool shed stood there before him in the corner of the garden, and he knew that his uncle and father had occasionally hidden things there they didn't want anyone to see, things that his cousin Hisafumi and he had discovered on more than one occasion when they were children. Once, they had even found a handgun hidden in a box of tools, something they had sworn never to divulge. His intuition began to speak to him again now, and it was this that convinced him to try his luck and investigate further. If there was something bad in there which might endanger his aunt and he did nothing about it, he knew he would never forgive himself.

Cautiously he advanced on the tool shed, and as quietly as possible, slid the old wooden latch aside and opened the door just enough to be able to see inside. As his eyes adjusted to the dark world of the tiny shed, he finally saw what had so obviously frightened his aunt and a wave of cold fear shot through his entire body.

In the shadowy interior of the little shed, gagged and firmly trussed hand and foot with strong climbing rope that his uncle used when he went to the mountains, were two men with hessian bags over their heads.

They were not moving.

Keiichi gasped, shut the door as quietly as he could and went rapidly back the way he had come up the side of the house to the main road.

He didn't see the big man with the buzz cut and the scowling face that was standing by his bicycle until it was too late. The man grabbed him powerfully by the arm as he raced through the gate and put him face-first on the ground before he could even think of reacting.

"Make a sound, make a move, and this is going to get unpleasant," the man whispered quietly in his ear.

====================

That evening the chief inspector arrived late at Penelope's house, and was pleased to see the light shining warmly in the windows. It had been a long and exhausting day after Nagano, and his nerves were on edge.

Penelope, trailed by a large black cat, opened the door and they went into the familiar living room where he had enjoyed so many meals over the years, and where she gave him a glass of cold white wine.

"You know, I am probably going to get myself fired over this, don't you Penny," he said quietly, sitting in his usual chair at the dining table and looking into her eyes.

She smiled at him and nodded. "I know. I was as surprised as you when you told me what Sal was planning."

"Yes, it's totally crazy. But he and Jun were insistent. I'm only sorry I couldn't bring you in on it earlier."

Yamashita said with a sigh. "I just wish there had been another way…."

She nodded. "What about Yokota? Have you told him anything?"

The chief inspector nodded.

"Yes, of course, he's in on it. We know the mole is someone connected to the *iaido-kendo* world, and Yokota *is* high up in that community and also very close to the case, so of course he was probably suspect number one. However, my gut tells me it's not him. We *will* find the bastard though, I promise you that."

"I know you will. So, the meeting is set?" asked Penelope.

"Yes. 10 a.m. If we do it any later, this whole thing could go south. It's only a matter of hours before he finds out what's happened, I'm pretty sure of that. Are you ready? You have the photograph?"

Penelope tapped her finger on a large manilla envelope on her table.

"Yes. One of his people has just driven all the way here with it. They've just left, actually."

Yamashita gestured at the file.

"Can I see it?"

"Of course."

Yamashita opened the envelope and held up the photograph.

"I can't really believe what I'm seeing…" he said reverently.

"Neither could I. But... there it is."
Yamashita handed her back the file and stood up. "I'll be here at eight-thirty to pick you up."

Chapter 19

The Jade Scroll

At exactly 10 a.m. Yamashita and Penelope presented themselves outside the elegant high-walled house in the leafy Shōtō area, home to many of the capital's wealthier and more famous families.

As they got out of the car, which was being driven by a uniformed officer who had been ordered to wait for them, Penelope surveyed the impressive villa.

"Well... it seems crime does pay," she said with a rueful smile. "I must have been misled...."

The chief inspector nodded. "More than I would care to admit."

They pressed the intercom, and a second later the wooden door in the huge traditional gateway swung open, and a smartly dressed man in a black suit stepped out to greet them.

"Hello, Tani-san. How's life?" asked Yamashita, much to Penelope's surprise.

The man smiled and bowed at the chief inspector.

"Ah... Yamashita-san. Nice to see you again, sir. You've come to see the boss, I gather?"

Yamashita told him they had, and the man politely ushered them inside, and they found themselves in a charming formal *karesansui* stone garden set before a large, traditional Japanese villa that looked like it had been extensively (and expensively) restored to its former glory of around a hundred years before.

As the man led them up to the doorway, Penelope touched Yamashita on the arm.

"You know him?" she whispered incredulously.

The chief inspector smiled.

"I probably know half his security staff. Most of them are ex-police," he whispered back. "I expect the pay is significantly better here."

Tani opened the front door of the house, where a woman in a dark kimono and white apron was waiting for them to take their shoes and offer them slippers.

Behind her in the entranceway, which had highly polished dark wood floors of Japanese old Japanese cypress, was an exquisite antique golden *byobu* folding screen featuring an autumn scene of people sitting under a maple tree watching the red and gold leaves falling around them while drinking sake.

"What a magnificent screen," said Penelope to the maid, who nodded and smiled modestly. Tani stepped past the woman and gestured for them to follow him.

They went quickly down a long and winding corridor, and Penelope had the chance to glimpse the serenely beautiful inner courtyard garden and some of the stately interior rooms.

"Wow..." she said. "This place is like some old aristocrats' manor house...."

"I think that's the idea he would like conveyed. You'll see what I mean," said Yamashita as they walked in an unhurried way through the house to where the corridor dead-ended in front of a large sliding door. Tani knocked twice before opening it, stepped to one side to let his guests enter, and then shut it wordlessly behind them.

They found themselves standing in a large tatami mat room with yet another gold folding screen, this time set behind a huge low table where three chairs were arranged, presumably for them and their host. The room looked out on the pond of the inner garden, where large white and red carp could be seen swimming underneath an old willow tree, which trailed its long green fronds elegantly above the still water.

The room seemed to radiate the calm peacefulness of bygone days, like it was a carefully constructed refuge from the outside world, where hustle and bustle and concern for material things had been firmly excluded. They also noticed next to the table a large ceramic *hibachi*, which seemed to be, but probably wasn't, the room's only source of heat against the chill of the late autumn morning, and which Penelope immediately recognized as the work of a famous Japanese ceramicist of the late Edo period. In the alcove there was also a beautiful decoration of seasonal pampas grass in a large red vase in front of a hanging scroll, which Penelope only had time to glance at and wished she could have examined more closely.

"I think if I had a room like this, I would never leave…" said Penelope wistfully.

"Yes… that's how I sometimes feel too…" said a deep bass voice in reply, the owner of which appeared as if by magic from an adjoining room.

Masakichi Bando, dressed as always in a dark *kimono*, gave them a low formal bow, the top of his bald head seeming to catch the morning light slightly as he did so. They then exchanged the usual polite greetings and introductions, and the old politician, who was tall with bushy eyebrows and a long, angular face, gestured for them to sit around the table with him. A moment later, as if on cue, the maid they had met at the entrance appeared with a tray of tea and a small kettle which she put on the top of the *hibachi* to keep warm.

"Please make yourselves comfortable. This tea is from a small farm my family has owned in Shizuoka for generations. I hope you enjoy it…" he said with a polite smile as the maid poured for them all.

"It's delicious," said Penelope, who held several licenses in the Japanese tea ceremony, which she had practiced her whole adult life.

Bando smiled at her.

"I see by the way you hold your cup that you are familiar with our customs," he said. "You have been in our country a long time?"

The way he said 'our' seemed calculated somehow to make her feel like a tourist who had dropped in while on a ten-day bus tour. Penelope thought about what to say, and decided it would be wise not to take the bait.

"Yes… a while now. What a beautiful house you have, Bando-*sensei*."

Bando smiled. "Thank you so much. It's also been in our family quite a while. I hear you used to work at Hassei university? And you, chief inspector - I hear that you are also from Kamakura?"

Yamashita glanced at Penelope and nodded at him in agreement. It was clear that the older man seemed to have been doing his homework on them.

"Yes, that's right. We both came up from Kamakura today to have this chat with you. Thank you for sparing the time."

Bando smiled and took a cigarette from a little silver box on the table and offered it to his guests, who refused, before lighting up himself with a tiny antique silver lighter. He had the confident demeanor of a man used to having a secure place in the world where he was universally admired, not to mention meticulously obeyed. He also had better manners than to question his guests as to why they were there, and was willing to wait until they told him, rather than give anything away.

"It's my pleasure. And I think the professor here actually hails from Britain, is that right?"

"Yes, that's right. Have you been there by chance?" asked Penelope amiably.

The older man waved a hand and smiled as if to indicate that was an impossible and perhaps even ridiculous idea.

"No, no, my dear. I find Japan has enough pleasures for one lifetime."

Yamashita and Penelope nodded, and there was silence between them for a moment, which Yamashita perhaps rather impatiently decided to break.

"I was wondering, *sensei,* if we could ask you some questions, perhaps?"

Bando raised a busy eyebrow.

"But of course, chief inspector. I must admit I was wondering when you were going to do that. I presume you are here on police business? And with your charming *foreign* friend... is she here on police business too?"

He gave Penelope a pleasant look, like she was one of the chief inspector's pets.

"Yes, that's right. Professor Middleton *is* here on police business. She's a departmental consultant of quite long standing, since you inquire..." said Yamashita testily.

Bando nodded innocently.

"Of course. And how may I assist the police and their... consultant?"

"That's kind of you, *sensei*," said Yamashita, giving a slight inclination of his head. "I was wondering if you could tell us a little about your parliamentary group. The *Shinenkai,* or New Flame Society, I believe it's called?"

Bando smiled, relaxed back into his chair, and folded his arms.

"The *Shinenkai*? Surely you know all about that. It's an intra-factional, inter-party group to promote traditional Japanese values. I don't think that's ever been much of a mystery. We have thousands of members, both in parliament and nationally. What else would you like to know?"

Yamashita looked him in the eye.

"Could you tell me what the group's position is on opening the imperial tombs for historical research?"

The older man slowly sat up straight.

"The imperial tombs? I don't think we have *any* policy on that. It's *government* policy, and the policy of the Imperial Household Agency. Which we fully support, of course, if that's what you mean..." he said evenly.

"Which is?"

Bando looked at him like a teacher looks at a child who hasn't done his homework.

"Which is that opening them would not only be a violation of the current law, which forbids it, but also a profanation of an imperial grave. Something no Japanese would ever consider, I'm sure," he said, looking at Penelope as if she could not possibly have anything to do with the conversation from this point on.

"I see. So tell me, *sensei*, do you think opening the pyramids is a profane act against the Egyptian kings?"

Bando laughed at this and shook his head. "Now chief inspector... Yamashita, is it? You know that's comparing apples with oranges. What the Egyptians choose to do with their ancient monarchs is up to them. We, on the other hand, are a little more civilized here. Would you like someone to open up *your* family grave for historical research? I think not..." he smiled.

"Well, I doubt my family grave is of much significance historically," said Yamashita. "However, I, for one, would like to know more about the history of my own country. And the truth or otherwise about what we teach our children in school. Wouldn't you?"

Bando took a sip of tea and looked into the dark green liquid in his cup as if there was an answer somewhere in it.

"This is a very curious topic to embark on so early in the morning, chief inspector. I must admit to being at a bit of a loss as to why you are here... No doubt what you say is true, history is very important...but we have to balance our curiosity sometimes..." he said.

"Against what, precisely?" asked Penelope, deciding not to be left out of the conversation any further.

"Against... respect. For one thing, professor," he said, looking at her as if she could not possibly grasp his meaning. "Respect for the imperial family. You've heard of them, I gather?" he said with a slight smirk.

"Ah yes... the imperial family. I have heard of them," said Penelope airily. "But it does seem that they, like you too, *sensei*, have some secrets you would rather people didn't pry into... Would that be fair to say?"

Bando drummed lightly on the highly polished table with his fingers like he was trying to control what came out of his mouth next and looked up at the ceiling for a moment.

"My life, dear professor, is an open book. I've spent all of it in the public, political sphere. I see no reason why their majesties need to do the same. We should protect them from any further... indignities, I feel. I'm sure even you would agree with that..." he replied coldly.

Yamashita nodded. "Well, whether or not we agree, *sensei*, that's not the issue. I think your group agrees with *you*, however. Wholeheartedly, in fact. And the issue we are here to talk about today is just how far you and your group would be willing to go to protect the imperial family from any... indignities...."

"Ah... so we arrive at the point of your visit then. Let me save you a little time then and answer your question. The *Shinenkai* would be willing to do anything *legal* to protect their majesties' reputation and peace of mind. And that's all I've got to say, I think.... Was there anything else?"

He sat back and took a sip of tea while looking out over the garden, where a small bird had just alighted on a rock next to the pond.

When he turned back to them, he saw a photograph that Yamashita had just placed in front of him. It was the one taken by Professor Xu's father of the team of murdered archaeologists.

Bando looked at it cursorily and looked back up at Yamashita with a confused look.

"I gather you know who these men were?" asked Yamashita pointedly.

Bando shrugged.

"You gather... *incorrectly*, chief inspector. I've never seen them before. Or this photograph, for that matter."

Yamashita nodded and gave a little smile.

"No, of course not. Let me fill you in, then. These men are all, *were* all, archaeologists. Experts on the subject of the Japanese imperial line."

"I see. Good for them," said Bando in a bored voice. "An excellent field of study. And your point is....?"

"My point is..." said Yamashita leaning forward and pointing to the photograph. "They are all dead."

There was silence for a moment, and Bando shifted his gaze between Penelope and the policeman.

"How unfortunate for them," he said.

"Yes, it is rather. Do you know why they are all dead?" asked Yamashita.

Bando smiled and raised his hands palms upward in a gesture of ignorance.

"They are dead, well... to be more accurate, *dead or disappeared*, it's the same thing really, because someone in your group thought they had trespassed inside a royal tomb while they were looking for the truth about the origins of the imperial family."

Bando looked up unconcerned, but his face betrayed a slight twitch under the eyes.

"A serious allegation, chief inspector. But... forgive me, I'm confused.... For your see, the truth about the royal family... is known already. These men, even if they did break the law as you imply, were in no danger of finding anything...other than what's already known."

Yamashita gave a significant glance at Penelope and then looked back at him.

"That's a very interesting way to phrase your response, Bando-*sensei*. It sounds like you *did* know them. Or at least *of* them...."

The older man smiled. "Chief inspector, you are free to surmise what you like."

Penelope leaned forward and looked him in the eye. "Tell me, *sensei*... wouldn't you like to know what they did find?"

Bando looked scared and visibly irritated for the first time during their meeting.

"And what was that?" he said with a frown.

Yamashita passed him another photograph, this time of the Teika Fragment. "Well... they found something mentioned in this document. A part of a letter by Teika-no-Fujiwara, the Heian period poet and historian. I think you are familiar with what that is, aren't you?"

Bando spent a moment quietly examining the document.

"And what if I am? It's not a crime to be aware of your country's history, at least the last time I checked. And, last time I did, no one had ever seen the object mentioned here."

Penelope reached into the file on her lap and put a large color photograph on the desk in front of the old politician.

"Are you sure of that, *sensei*?" she said quietly.

Bando stared aghast at the photograph.

"What is this?!" his voice shaking with rage.

Penelope nodded to the photograph. It showed a long table in a large tatami mat room with a huge cloth scroll made of up bars of green jade sewn into a silk backing unrolled across it. It stretched for several meters along the table, and was clearly of great age.

"This *sensei*, is the Jade Scroll. The one you say does not exist. It is the earliest extant record of the imperial line, written by the Chinese court historian Yen-su in the fourth century BC. This is the document that Teika-no-Fujiwara was holding over the head of the then Emperor Go-Toba in the thirteenth century. Would you like to know what it says?" she asked icily. "I think you would, since you have killed so many people to stop it from seeing the light of day…."

"It's probably a fake or a forgery. You have no evidence that this is real, nor that anything written on it is true."

Penelope smiled.

"That's true. I don't. But the late Professor Suzuki… he *did* have the evidence. Although he had not seen the scroll itself, he had confirmed the story it told from other Chinese sources. A comprehensive analysis that proves what the Scroll says is accurate, taken from an ancient Chinese commentary. Something that Go-Toba obviously knew as well."

Bando snorted in disgust. "And what is that, pray?"

Penelope cocked her head to one side. "Oh, come now, *sensei*. I think you know full well what it says. That long ago, a son of a Chinese emperor came to Japan with a large armed force, and took over the lands that his father had bequeathed to him in a settlement with the vassal kings of the Yamato plain, and became the first emperor of Japan. His name was Jin-mu. Known today, of course, as Jimmu. Although now, thanks to the Scroll, we know he is not legendary anymore. He was, in fact… *real*."

Bando looked up at her furiously.

"That… is a lie!" he screamed at her. "Now… get out of my house!"

Yamashita leaned forward and smiled at him.

"Oh, just a moment, *sensei*. Don't you want to hear the rest? Your friend Katayama-san was quite interested when we told him. He's down at the station at the moment… in a holding cell. With his friends… the Odawara brothers…."

Bando glared at him, but said nothing.

Yamashita smiled at him tauntingly.

"You see this photograph of the archaeologists? The one you claim never to have seen before? Well, we found a copy of it in your friend Katayama's office, which he kindly explained you had given to him. These were the men we now know *you* ordered killed for breaking into an imperial tomb looking for *this*…" he tapped his finger on the picture of the Scroll.

"But the truth is… interjected Penelope. "That you didn't know which tomb, nor where it was… did you? You just knew they had found something…and that was all the information you needed."

"This is nonsense. Complete nonsense," said Bando. "And I will be taking up this matter with the Justice Ministry...."

Yamashita ignored him and carried on. "So, back to your friend Katayama-san and the Odawara boys. They were singing like birds after we told them the reality of what they had done... You see, those men don't mind killing if it's all about the *cause*... as you call it. But when it comes to getting the death penalty for something that *wasn't* about the cause... that's a different issue. Because you see, *sensei*... this picture of the archaeologists... was taken in *China*."

Bando looked at him uncomprehendingly.

"China?" he whispered.

"At a dig run by the late Professor Xu, of the national university in Hunan. Where they found conclusive evidence that confirms the story of the Scroll...in a *Chinese* tomb...."

Bando swore under his breath.

"Anything to say?" asked Penelope with a smile.

Bando sat back in his chair and folded his arms.

"Nothing. Is there anything else *you* would like to say? Anything else, before I presume you arrest me? Which would be a *very large mistake* on your part, believe me, chief inspector...."

Yamashita nodded.

"Actually, there is. But first, I have a question for you. Be careful how you answer it now...."

The older man sighed. "Go on."

"I'm going to let my friend Professor Middleton ask you, if you don't mind."

Bando shifted his gaze to Penelope, and she asked him quietly,

"Are you a patriot, *sensei*? Do you believe in your cause?"

Bando shot her a curious look.

"Of course. You know that," he said flatly.

"Good," she said calmly. "How would you like *not* to get the death penalty, and also for the existence of the Scroll to remain secret?"

Bando's eyes opened wide and Penelope saw real fear light in them.

"Go on then. What's the deal?"

"Simple," she said. "Confess to the killings of these men." She tapped on the picture of the murdered archaeologists. "The two men you ordered kidnapped were found safe at the home of the elder Odawara brother, and are safe. You'll be charged with their kidnapping as well. And we want the name of your mole in the police force. Tell us the whole story, and the Scroll stays hidden. And Professor Suzuki's research also remains secret. Your cause stays safe. And all the fake history you love so much, you get to keep it. Everyone does. That's the deal."

Bando seemed to choke on his breath.

"And how do I know you will keep your word?" he hissed.

Penelope reached forward and tapped the photograph of the Scroll.

"You don't," she said quietly. "But as a patriot, as the leader of your cause, you might want to consider what your legacy is going to be if the truth comes out. I'd take the risk, if I were you, because at this point, you don't have very much else to lose. Chief Inspector Yamashita here is going to arrest you at the end of this meeting, and the scandal is going to kill the *Shinenkai* as a political force forever. But... if you care about the 'official version' of history, that's the only thing you can preserve, and that's the only thing that's on the table. You can take it or leave it, but the offer is void the moment we stand up."

Chapter 20

Lost Kingdom

Sal poured them a glass of wine while Penelope served them her *poulet au vin blanc*, which was from an old recipe handed down in her family for many years and that she had been simmering all day on her stovetop in readiness for tonight's little party.

It was just a week after the arrest of Bando Masakichi and his group, an event that had made headlines across the country, and she had invited everyone involved for a small celebration and also the first chance to meet with Sal and Jun Miyamoto, who had been found unharmed at the Odawara house after their brief imprisonment that had been monitored from the beginning by a police S.W.A.T. team supervised by Yamashita and his detective sergeant.

Chief Inspector Yamashita, who for some reason was always a favorite perch for all of Penelope's four cats, placed Alphonse, her large black tomcat, gently on the ground and raised his glass to the others.

"Well, here's to all of you. We couldn't have cracked this without you, that's for sure…."

Professor Xu, Fei, and Sachie all raised their glasses and smiled.

"So…" began Professor Xu. "What do you think is going to happen? I'm not an expert on the Japanese judicial system, but I imagine the consequences will be pretty dire for them."

Yamashita gave her a rueful smile. "Believe me, I wish I weren't an expert, I might be more optimistic. With people like Bando, things are going to be difficult. Yes, we have a confession of sorts, thanks to Penelope, but I think the truth is that he will die in prison even if they give him capital punishment. He's already over eighty. I think that's the most likely outcome. Probably the same for Katayama. As for the Odawaras… they might not be so lucky… They already have form for violent assault. But if they fight it… who knows. I'm pretty sure Bando and especially Katayama will not hesitate to throw them under the bus if push comes to shove, though."

"And what about the *Shinenkai*?" asked Fei.

Yamashita shook his head. "I dunno about them. You probably know more about that than me," he said taking a sip of wine and no doubt referring to Fei's voracious daily consumption of news media. "However, I would bet a case of Kirin beer they will simply drum up a new guy to lead them and carry straight on. That's how things usually roll in Nagatacho in my experience."

Penelope finished serving the food, and silence fell for a while as they all ate.

"This is really good," said Sachie. "What is it? My aunt used to make something like this I think…but it wasn't this nice."

Penelope nodded. "Yes, actually it's a recipe from *my* aunt, or rather my great, great aunt... I got it via my mother, and she got it from her mother, who was French...."

"I've had it before... *poulet*, right? I never get tired of it..." said Sal smiling. "So, anyway, I've got a question, if you don't mind."

Penelope smiled. "I bet I know what it is. The Scroll?"

Jun looked up. "Actually, that was my question too. I'm dying to see it. You have no idea how many questions it's going to answer...."

Sal nodded. "Precisely. The Scroll. When do we get to see it?"

"He's not the only one," said Professor Xu eagerly. "For my father's sake... he would have been so excited... I think he would have started dancing...."

Penelope looked at everybody gathered around the table, and at Yamashita, who looked at the floor, and quietly hated herself for what she was about to tell them.

"The answer is... I don't know. That was the deal I made with the abbot. The Scroll will stay hidden, and even the photograph he sent us that we used to get Bando to give us information... that's been destroyed, as per his request."

"You mean... you never saw it?"

Penelope shook her head.

"Never. I have no idea where it is, either. Only the abbot knows that. They were not willing to release it to the public at this time, as they think it's still too dangerous. And given the current turn of events... I kind of agree with them," she said sadly. "But when I explained what had happened… he *was* willing to help, but only in a limited way.

"So… you lied to him. To Bando…." said Fei, with a slight smile.

"Yes. She did. With my help, I might add," said Yamashita with a smile. "She's actually a master of the Art of the Bluff. Whatever you do, don't play cards with her."

"Yeah, I kind of remember saying that myself once…." said Sal.

Jun sat looking despondent with his head in his hands.

"Are you OK, Miyamoto-san?" asked Sachie, giving the younger man a concerned look.

Jun looked up slowly.

"I'm just thinking about Professor Suzuki's research… without the Scroll…."

Professor Xu leaned forward and said sadly, "I know… I understand what you are saying. Without the Scroll, it can't be confirmed. His research was based on my father's, which also cannot be confirmed now. It will remain just a story in an old Chinese commentary, and some etchings on a piece of jade…."

"Well," said Fei, "At least you can take comfort from the fact that he was right on the money. It was all true."

Jun sighed. "I know. But until the Scroll is made public, until we can study it… it'll all just remain a theory."

Penelope reached across and patted him on the hand.

"It was a deal we had to make. To get justice for those killed and for their families… The abbot saw that too, that's why he offered to help."

"That's true," said Yamashita. "You guys took an enormous risk."

Sal and Jun exchanged a glance and looked at the floor.

"You lured the Odawara brothers after you from Nagasaki, knowing they were on to you… and then you allowed them to kidnap you so you could incriminate them…."

Sal nodded. "Yeah, I figured it out on the way. They must have known where I was in order for them to turn up there so fast. It didn't take me long to find the tracker. I thought the only way we were going to catch them in the act of something criminal was to let them take us at my house, and then to let Yamashita-san here and his folk arrest them. Fortunately, Jun agreed to go along with it."

"It was the least I could do for Professor Suzuki…." Jun said quietly. "But it was very touch and go at some points."

"Why? What happened?" asked Fei.

Yamashita shook his head.

"Well, as you know, we had a mole in the police force who was updating Katayama, and through him the Odawaras, as to what we were doing, so we were very limited in whom we could trust to do what Sal was asking. This was another key thing we managed to get out of Bando – the identity of the mole, who turned out to be a junior officer who had family connections to the Odawaras. Anyway, in the end, I got onto an old police tech I have known for many years who was able to rendezvous with them on their way to Nagano and fit some tiny trackers in their shoes, so we knew where they were at all times. What we did not know was whether the Odawara brothers were not going to kill them the moment they found them, though. However, Sal was right, they were obviously after the flash drive with Professor

Suzuki's research and would have failed if they returned without it. Jun stalled them by telling them it was in a safety deposit box at a bank, so that basically stopped them in their tracks, and they decided to wait until they had a meeting with Katayama to get the green light as to what to do. The tactical team had followed them at a distance, so after they left in the morning, we moved into the house to wait for them and to make sure Sal and Jun were OK. But then the son turned up and got suspicious. We didn't know if he had spotted the police in the house with the aunt, which actually he hadn't, as it turned out. Fortunately, Yokota's friend on the S.W.A.T team was quick enough to grab him, or God knows who he might have told…."

"So, you arrested them…."

"Yes, at Katayama's office when they turned up. Once we had all of them, we only had to get Bando to confess. Of course, we wanted him to confess to nabbing Sal and Jun here as well… so we had to keep it quiet. If nothing else, we have the Odawara boys dead to rights for kidnapping and attempted murder. That should be enough, even if we can't prove the rest."

Yamashita slapped Sal on the knee.

"I'm just grateful we were able to get to you on time. We badly underestimated the brothers, you know. They were no fools when it came to surveillance. And when we nabbed them, Katayama and the brothers said nothing at all. Until they realized that we had recovered you both and that Bando had given in and confessed. Then they sang like songbirds."

Fei smiled. "I still can't believe the Odawara brothers talked. Those guys seemed pretty tough."

Yamashita laughed. "Like a lot of people like them, they are not as tough as they think. When my detective sergeant told them he was going to arrest the younger brother's son, Keiichi, as an accessory, he gave up his older brother in a blink. And himself. There you go, I suppose, that's families…"

"What about the tomb? Was that really in China? And the jade you found?" asked Jun.

"Absolutely," said Professor Xu. "My father took that picture. All those men, including Sal's uncle, were his friends and colleagues. He'd asked them to come to China with Professor Nakamura to help him with the dig, which was quite an important one. And it was Sal's uncle who found the jade which was later recovered from that temple on Mt. Haguro. He took it back to Japan with my father's permission for research purposes. He and my father were ecstatic at the time because it seemed to confirm this new story about the imperial line in Japan, a story which they believed Teika no Fujiwara was fully informed about because he had the Scroll… a completely different version of Japanese history than what has been handed down. The jade Sal's uncle found was in a burial mound belonging to an ancient court historian from the early Tang period who also had briefly recorded the exploits of the emperor's son, Jin-mu, who went to Japan on his father's orders to take control of the country and supervise tribute from the Japanese vassal kings. Of course, when Bando and the *Shinenkai* heard of it being in Professor Nakamura's possession and found that photograph, they assumed it had been taken from an imperial tomb here in Japan. What else were they going to think? Bando and the *Shinenkai* had people monitoring the archaeological world for decades, making sure that as far as possible that the imperial tombs stayed shut off from research so that there was nothing that might threaten the accepted version of the imperial story. He was well aware of the Teika Fragment and the Scroll and was adamant that nothing ever be done to find it. Which was why, of course, he took out each of the archaeologists in that picture. When he heard about Professor Suzuki's research…that sent him into another panic. Until Penny-*sensei* found the jade and started to put two and two together, he must have thought he was safe."

"Wasn't just getting Katayama to confess enough, though? That would have been enough for a court to send his boss down, right?" asked Sachie.

Yamashita stared at his wine.

"Yes, that's true. We had a strong case, but only Bando knew the details about everything. We needed to get the kingpin, that was the only way we could maybe get justice for all those men who had died so long ago. But we would never have got him to do so without the Scroll. That was the *only* thing that would have made him trade information."

"Because he was just a fanatic in the end. That was the truth," said Sachie.

Penelope nodded. "Yes. That was true for him. He wasn't a liar. He believed all the nonsense he talked."

"Which brings me to my question," said Fei. "What on earth did you say to the abbot to make him give you a picture of something his family had kept an absolute secret for eight hundred years? That must have been a good story."

Sachie smiled and looked up.

"Yeah, I was involved in that bit. We both went to see him a second time. He knows me, and he respects Penny-*sensei* and what she told him. We just told him the truth. That lives were at stake unless we could convince Bando that the Scroll really existed. After that, he was happy to help. He regarded it as his duty as a Buddhist priest. Life, after all, is more important than history… that's what he said."

"But releasing the Scroll…" said Jun, who still looked disappointed.

"That was a step too far for him," said Penelope calmly. "At least for the moment…."

"OK," said Fei with a confused look. "But how did you convince Bando that you would keep your promises?

"Well," said Penelope, "that was always the question. But Bando had no choice but to trust us, even if he didn't. It was his one and only chance to 'preserve imperial dignity.' That's what I told him anyway. I said that the Scroll had been protected for almost a millennium by people that really did not want to release it unless there was *a threat to human life*…. And that whether it stayed that way depended completely on whether he was prepared to face justice. It was something he understood, it seems."

Sal smiled. "And here we are… Of course, Jun here still has Professor Suzuki's research. They never got their hands on that."

"You mean the flash drive you told me about when you were driving back to Nagano?" asked Yamashita.

Jun nodded and laughed. "Yeah. That was it. I managed to hide that just before they snatched us at Sal's place."

"Ah…I was wondering about that. I assumed they must have got hold of it. The forensic tech's turned that cottage upside down. No flash drive. Where did you put it?"

"Oh, there was some old tree stump out the front of the house which Sal used to chop wood. I put it in one of the cracks. It was still there when we went back for it," said Jun.

"A tree stump?" asked Yamashita.

"Yeah. Why?"

The chief inspector finished his wine and as he placed the glass back on the table, Penelope's large black cat seized the chance and returned to curl up on his lap.

Yamashita smiled and rolled his eyes.

"Oh… It's just because I was sitting on that stump the other day. Whoever knew trees held so much history…."

About the Author

Ash Warren is an Australian author who graduated with a degree in medieval history and English literature from the University of New South Wales in Sydney.

After a period of roaming the world with a backpack, he settled in Japan, where he has now lived since 1992. During that time he has written and published widely on language and Japanese culture, and teaches at a university in Tokyo.

He is the author of The Penelope Middleton series: *Dark Tea, The Quiet Game,* and also of *The Way of Salt: Sumo and the Culture of Japan* (Silman-James Press, Los Angeles), *The Language Code,* and *Mastering the Japanese Writing System.* (Also available at Amazon and elsewhere.)

He lives with his family in Tokyo with one dog, two cats and has a penchant for chess, sumo, classical music, and talking about politics over too much sake.

The Penelope Middleton Series

The Singing Blade is the third book in the Penelope Middleton series and follows:

Dark Tea
The Quiet Game

If you would like to be updated about further books in the series and other books by the author, please go to:

www.arwarren.net

and subscribe!

If you would like to contact the author directly, please write to:

wslc2000@hotmail.com

Printed in Great Britain
by Amazon